JAKE MADDOX
GRAPHIC NOVELS

# STRANGE BOARDERS

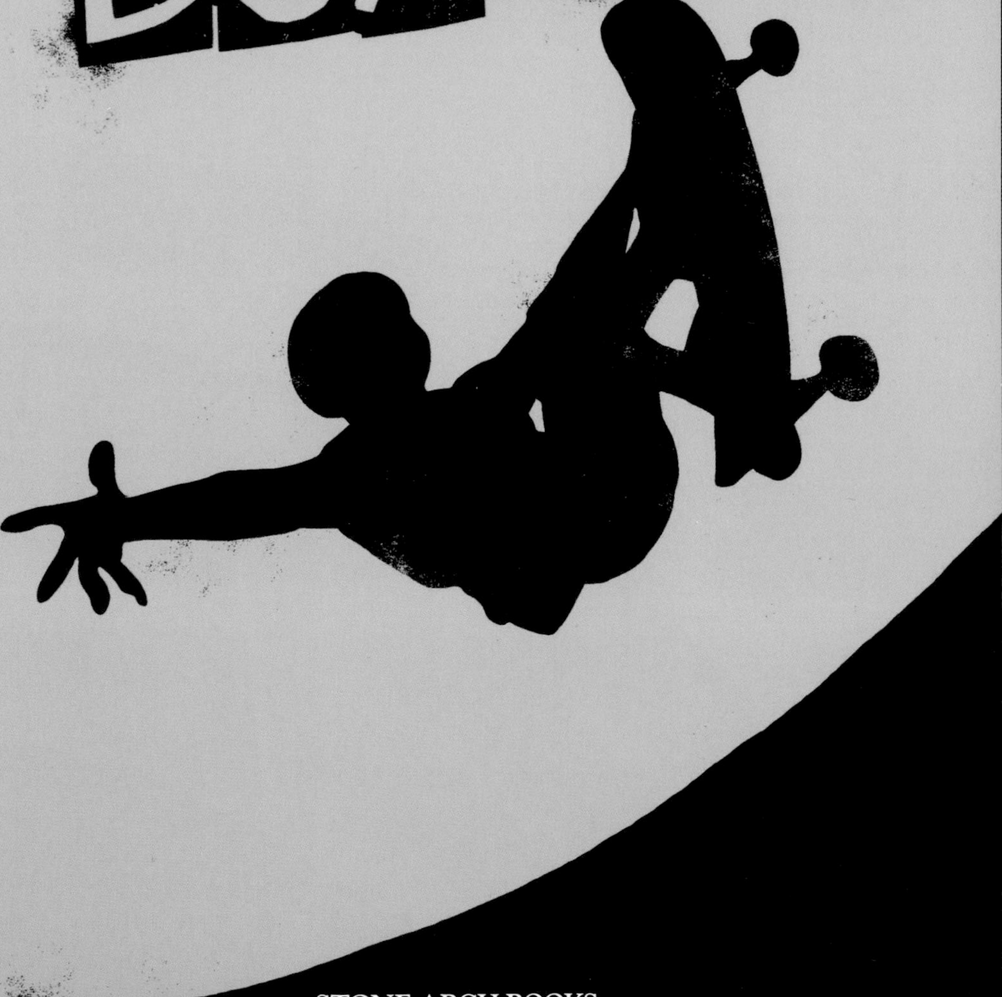

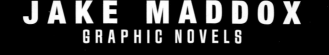

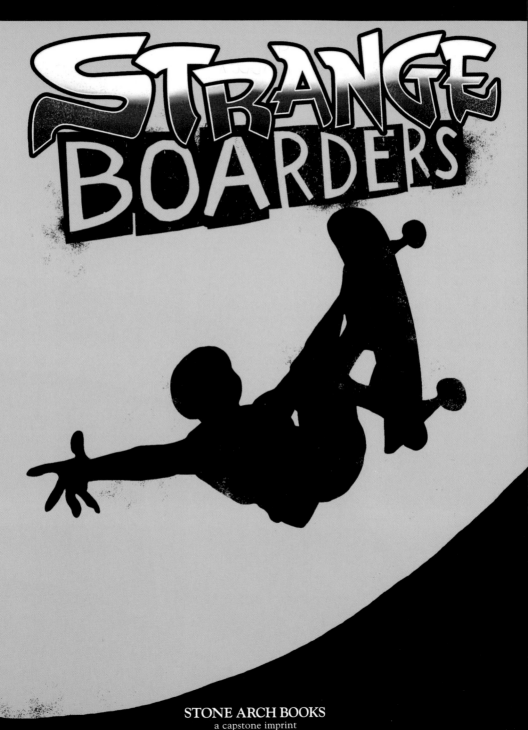

STONE ARCH BOOKS
a capstone imprint

# JAKE MADDOX
## GRAPHIC NOVELS

Jake Maddox Graphic Novels are published by
Stone Arch Books, a Capstone imprint
1710 Roe Crest Drive
North Mankato, Minnesota 56003

www.mycapstone.com

J
GN
MADDOX

11|19

Library of Congress Cataloging-in-Publication Data
is available on the Library of Congress website at
https://lccn.loc.gov/2018005698

ISBN 978-1-4965-6046-9 (library binding)
ISBN 978-1-4965-6050-6 (paperback)
ISBN 978-1-4965-6054-4 (eBook PDF)

Summary: Recently resettled in America, Adnan Zakaria
is a Syrian refugee whose skateboarding skills are the only
thing that allows him to connect with the other kids in
his neighborhood. But when his skateboard disappears
and turns up in the hands of local troublemaker Mike
Proctor, Adnan has to out-skate his foe to win it back.

Editor: Aaron Sautter
Designer: Brann Garvey
Production Specialist: Tori Abraham

Printed in the United States of America.
PA021

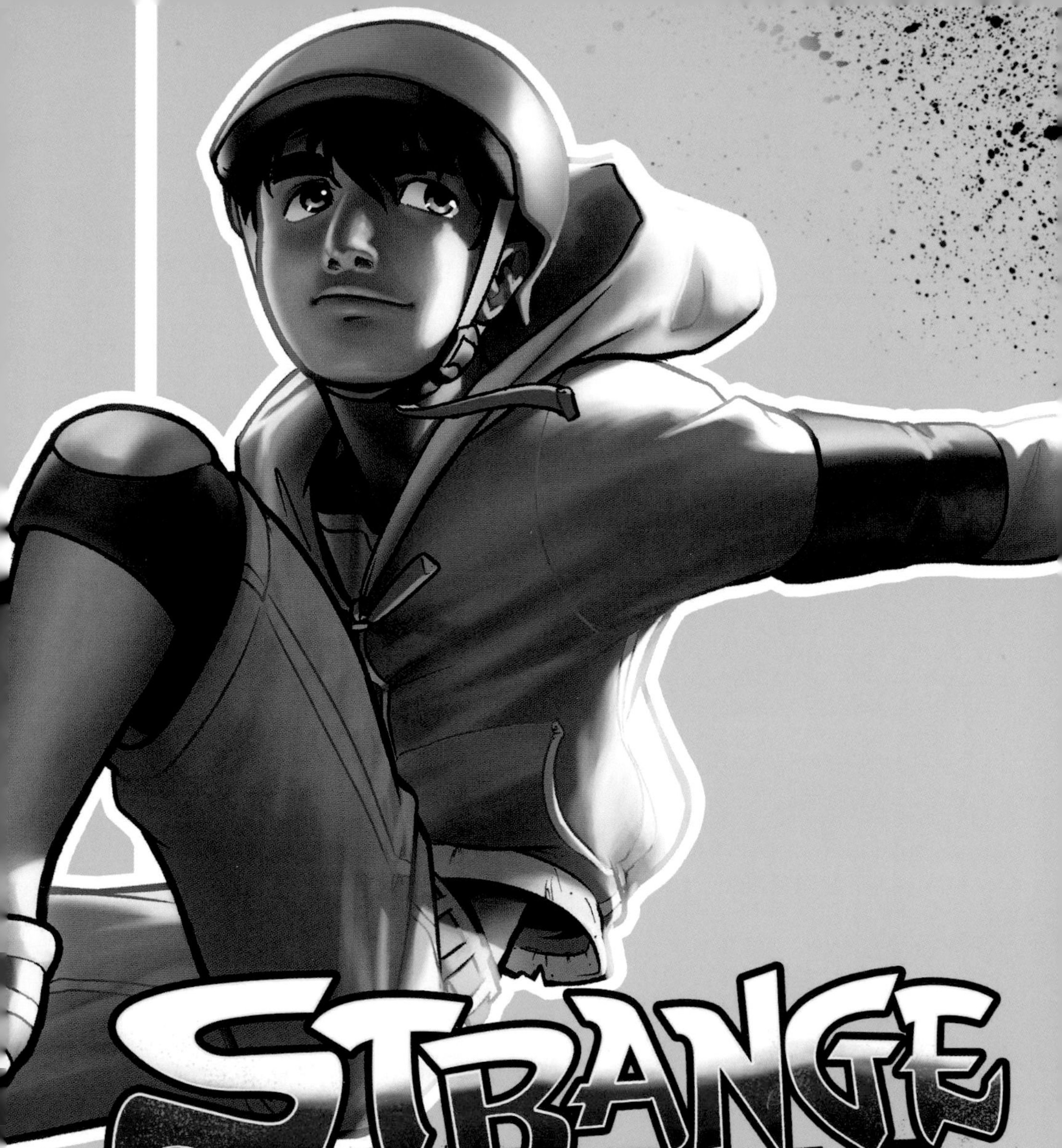

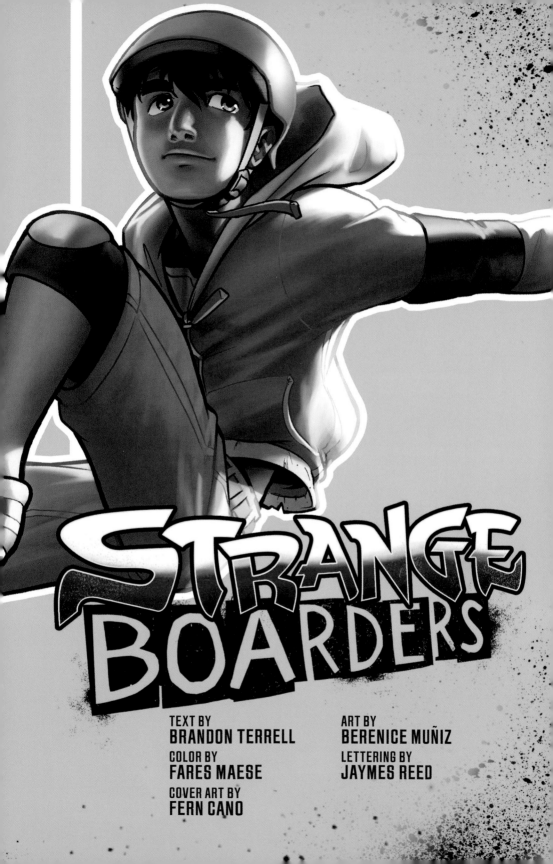

# STRANGE BOARDERS

TEXT BY
BRANDON TERRELL

ART BY
BERENICE MUÑIZ

COLOR BY
FARES MAESE

LETTERING BY
JAYMES REED

COVER ART BY
FERN CANO

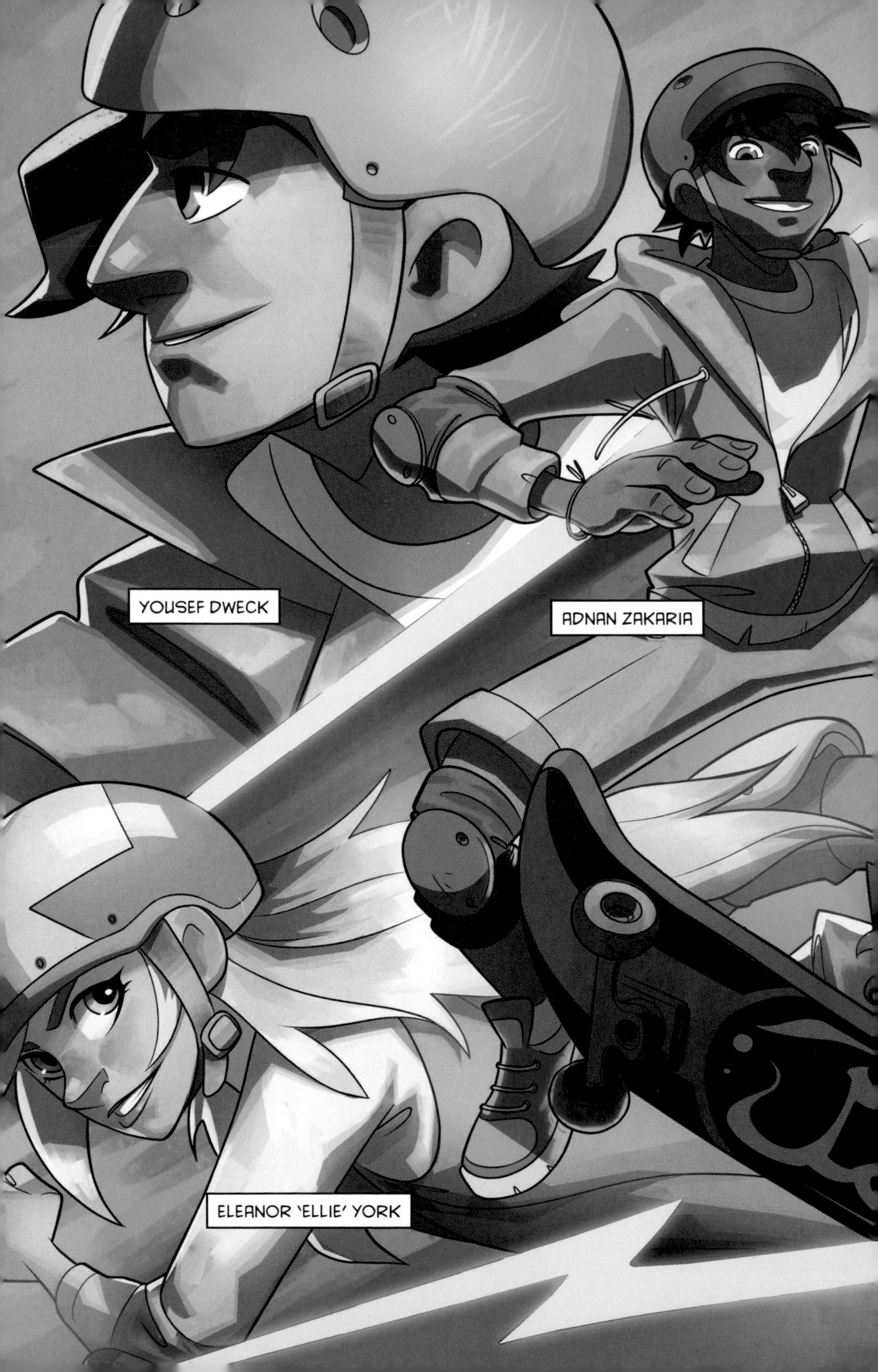
YOUSEF DWECK
ADNAN ZAKARIA
ELEANOR 'ELLIE' YORK

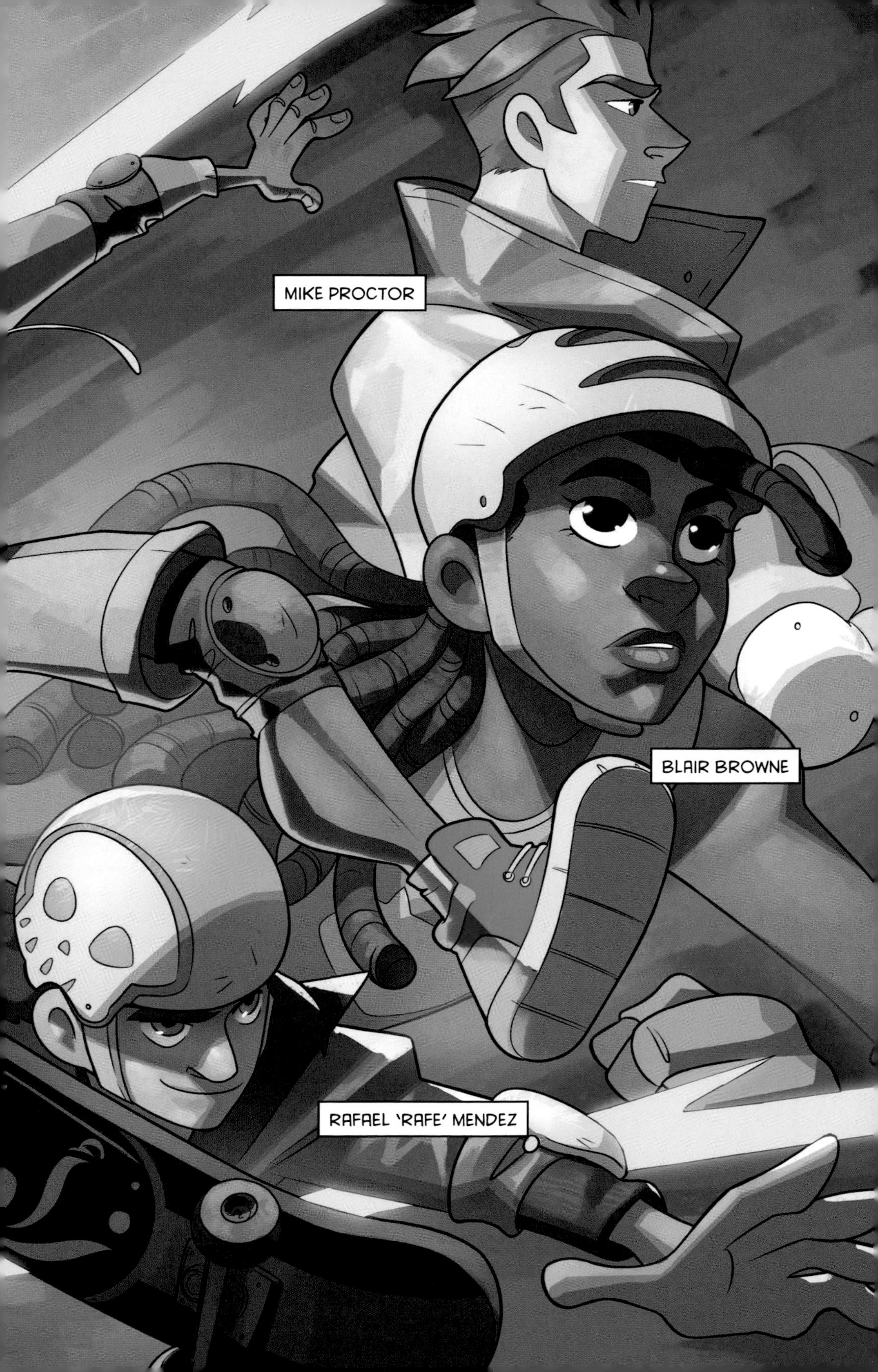
MIKE PROCTOR
BLAIR BROWNE
RAFAEL 'RAFE' MENDEZ

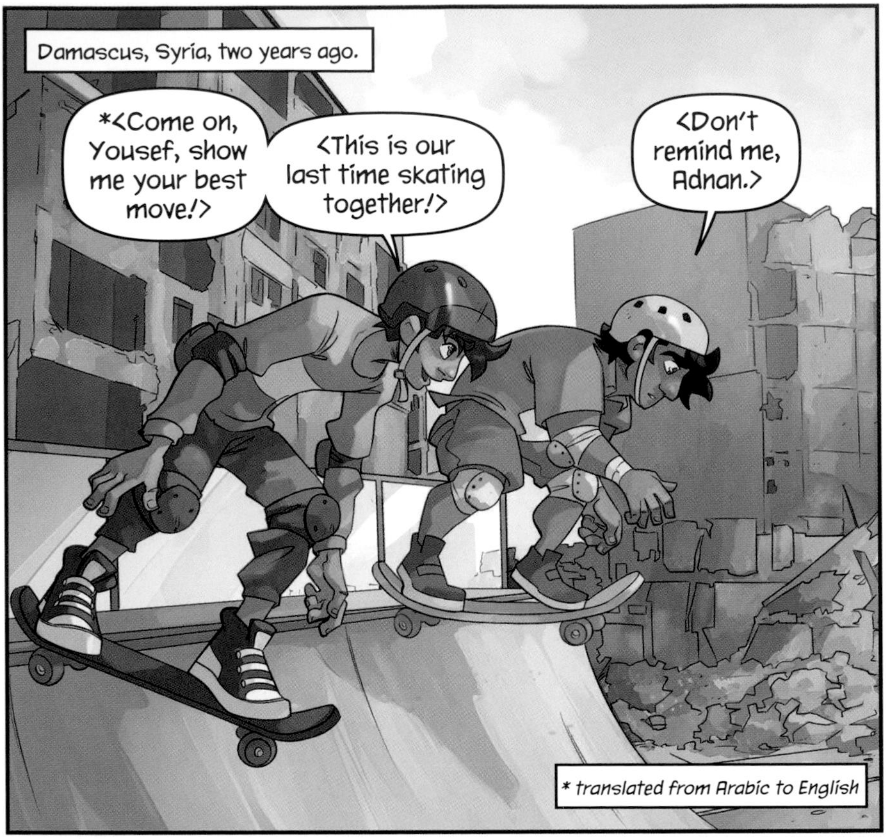
Damascus, Syria, two years ago.
*<Come on, Yousef, show me your best move!>
<This is our last time skating together!>
<Don't remind me, Adnan.>
* translated from Arabic to English

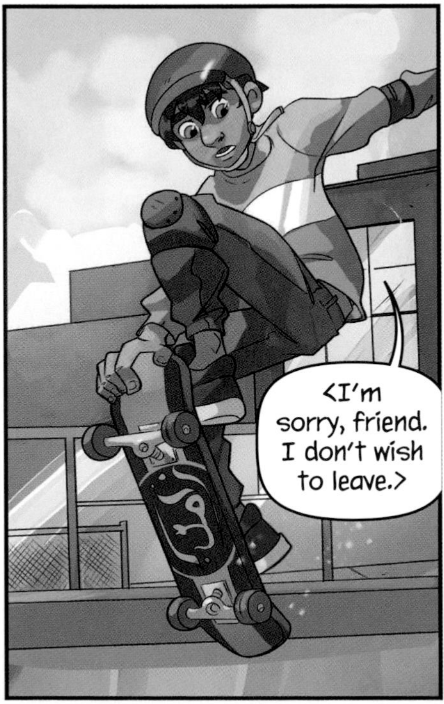
<I'm sorry, friend. I don't wish to leave.>

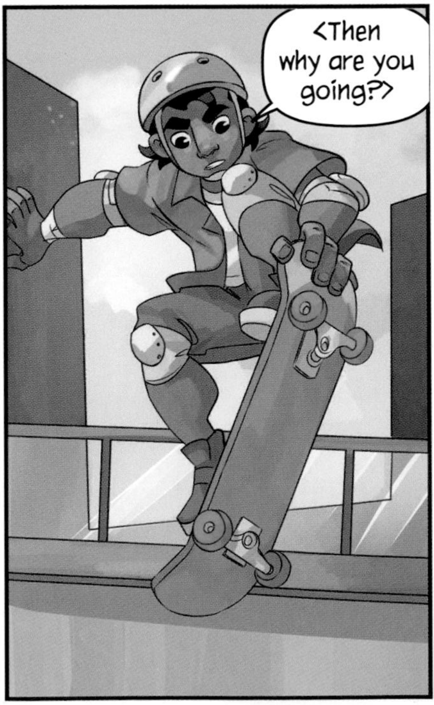
<Then why are you going?>

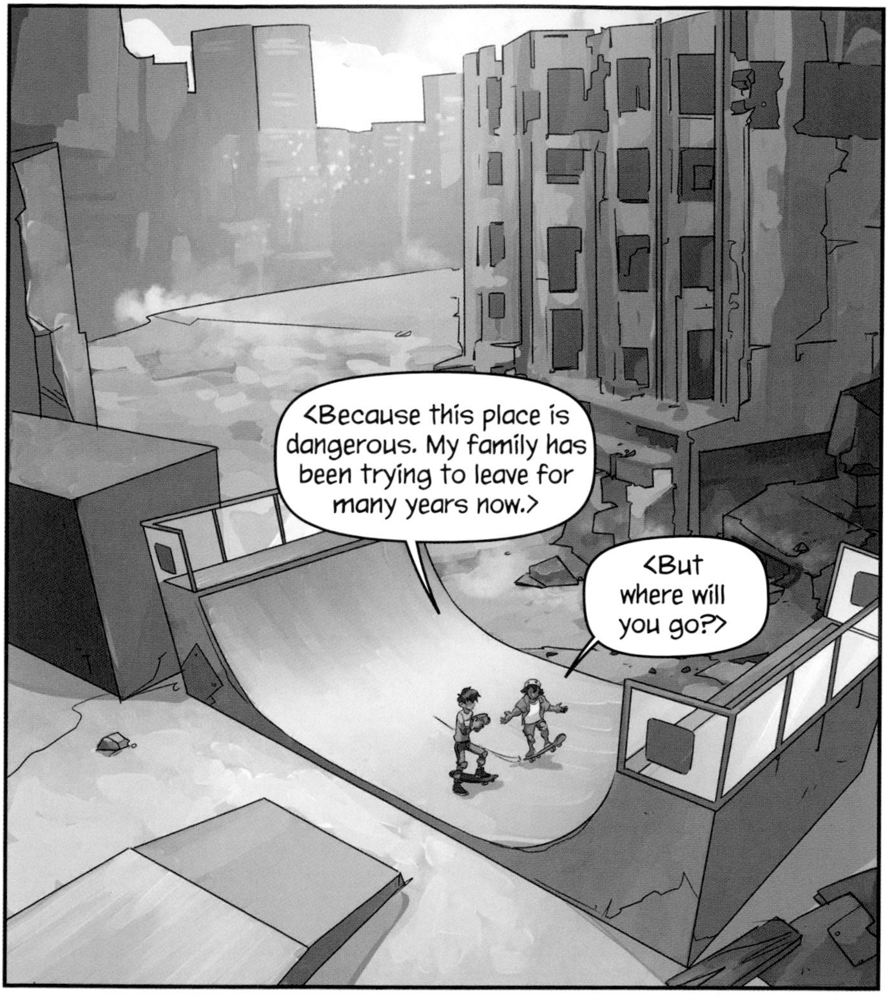
<Because this place is dangerous. My family has been trying to leave for many years now.>
<But where will you go?>

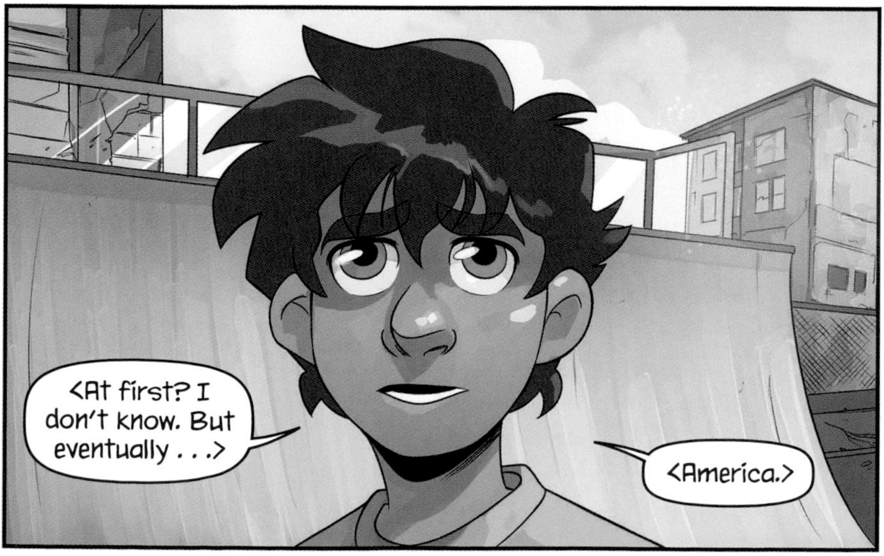
<At first? I don't know. But eventually . . .>
<America.>

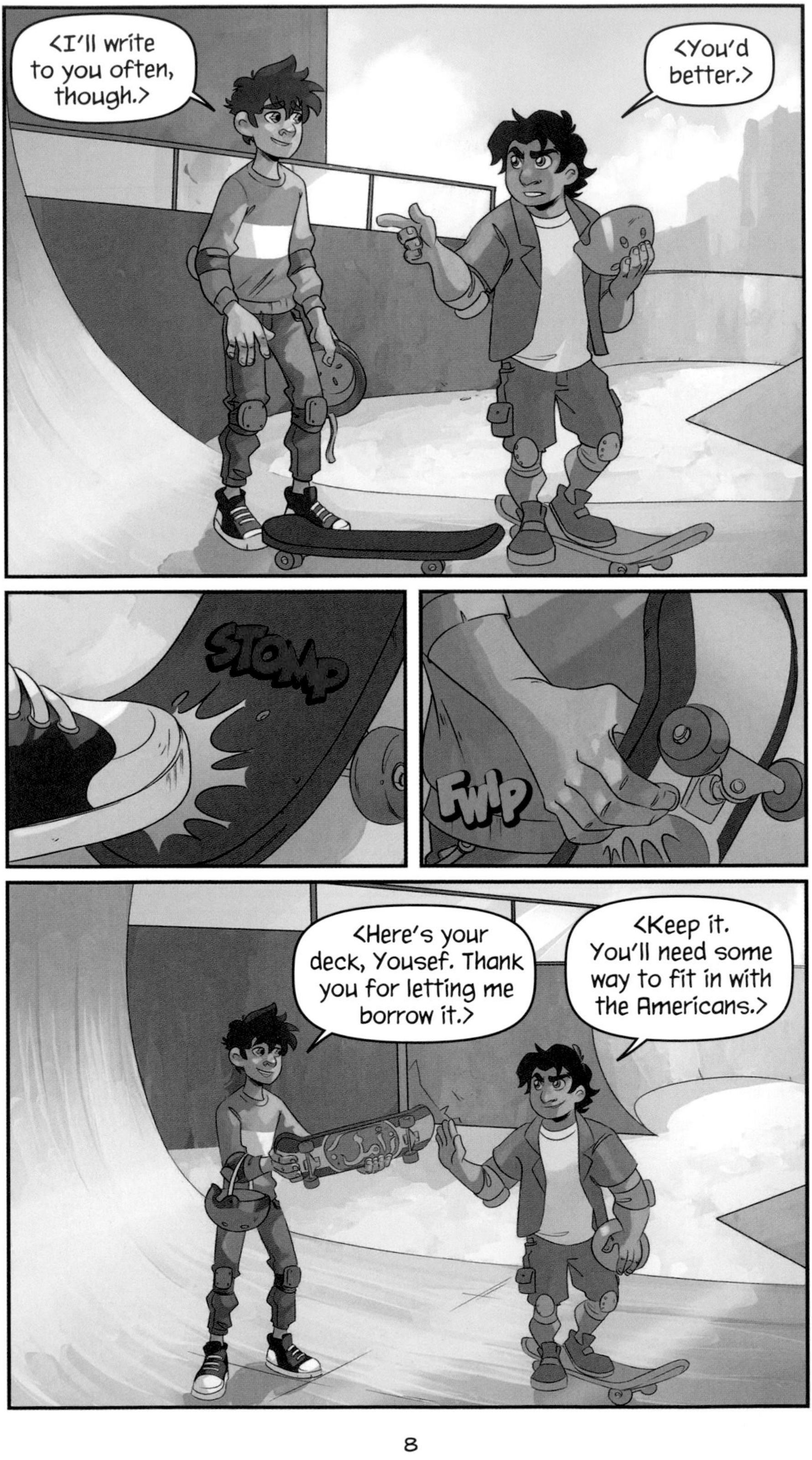
<I'll write to you often, though.>
<You'd better.>
STOMP
FWIP
<Here's your deck, Yousef. Thank you for letting me borrow it.>
<Keep it. You'll need some way to fit in with the Americans.>

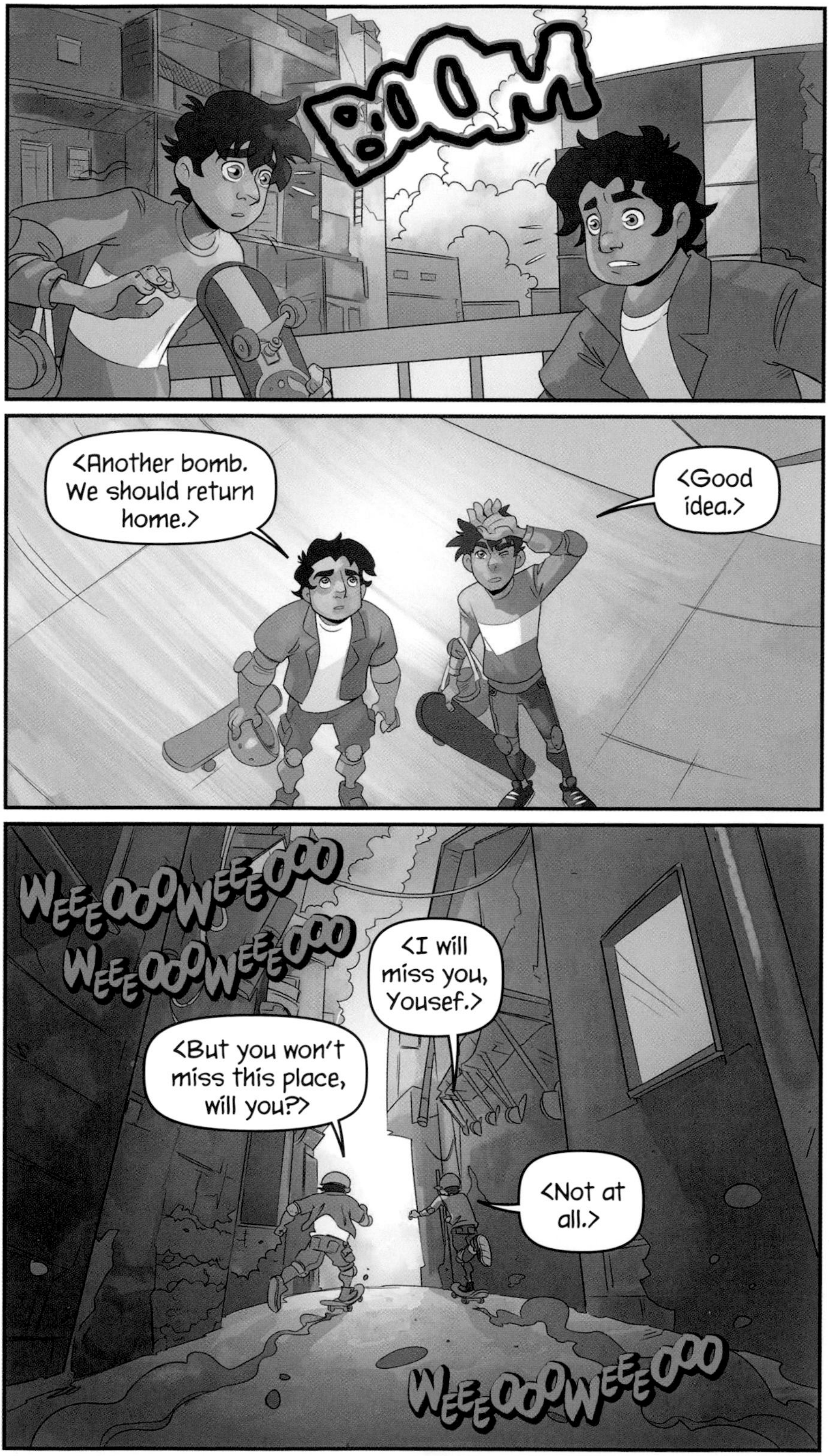
BOOM
<Another bomb. We should return home.>
<Good idea.>
WEEEOOOWEEEOOO
WEEEOOOWEEEOOO
<I will miss you, Yousef.>
<But you won't miss this place, will you?>
<Not at all.>
WEEEOOOWEEEOOO

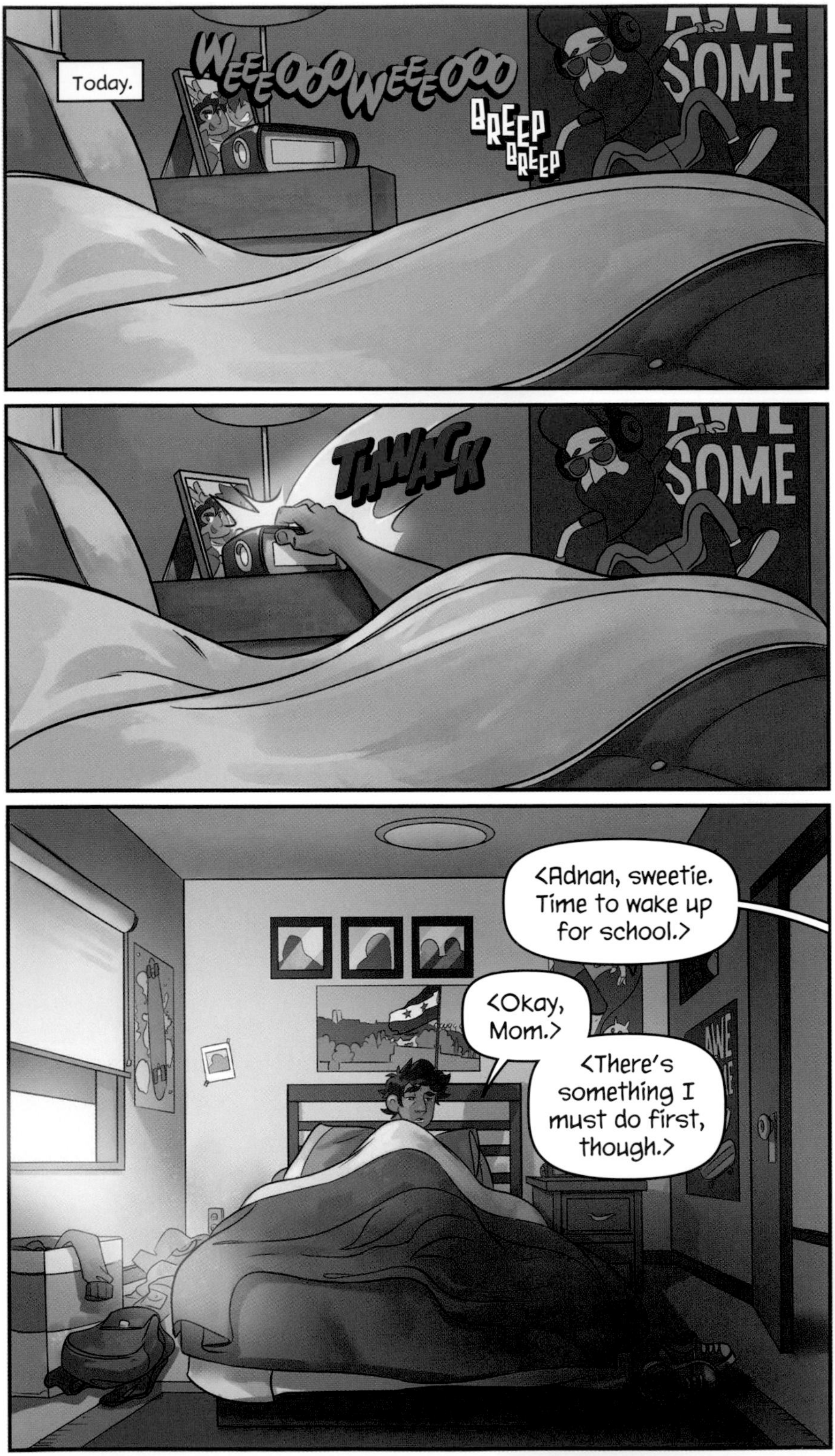
Today.
WEEEOOOWEEEOOO
BREEP
BREEP
SOME
THWACK
SOME
<Adnan, sweetie. Time to wake up for school.>
<Okay, Mom.>
<There's something I must do first, though.>

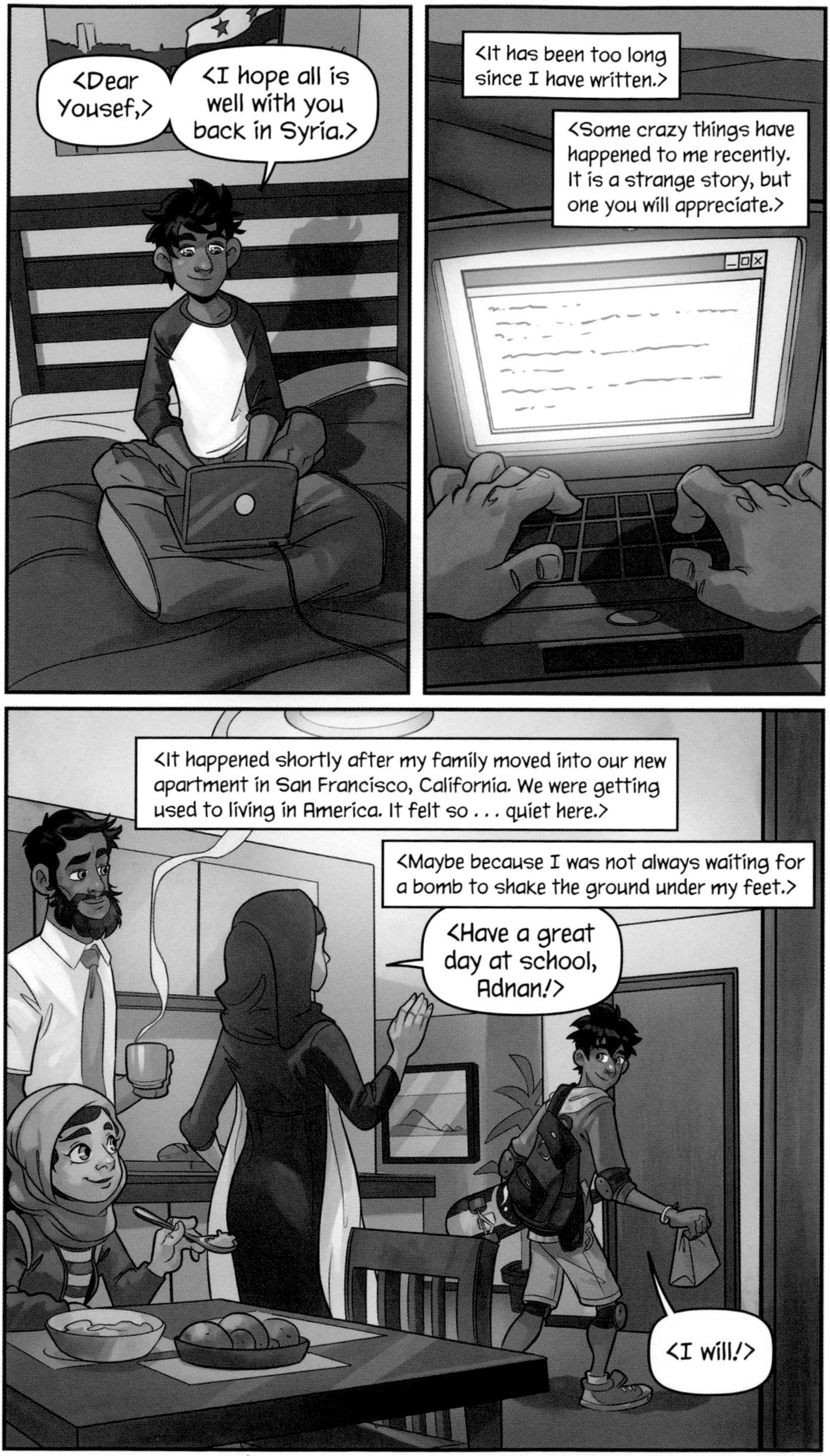
<Dear Yousef,>
<I hope all is well with you back in Syria.>
<It has been too long since I have written.>
<Some crazy things have happened to me recently. It is a strange story, but one you will appreciate.>
<It happened shortly after my family moved into our new apartment in San Francisco, California. We were getting used to living in America. It felt so . . . quiet here.>
<Maybe because I was not always waiting for a bomb to shake the ground under my feet.>
<Have a great day at school, Adnan!>
<I will!>

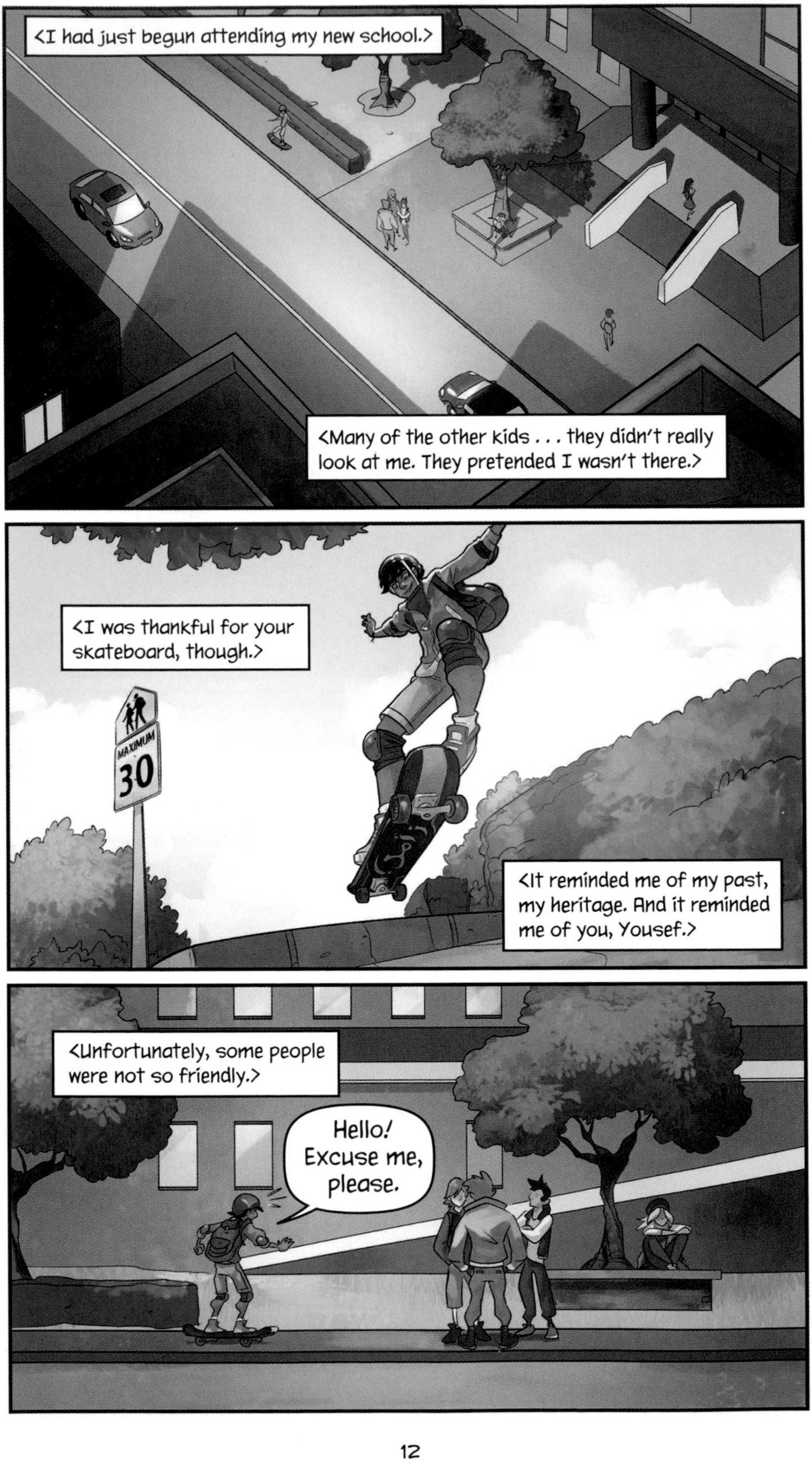
<I had just begun attending my new school.>
<Many of the other kids . . . they didn't really look at me. They pretended I wasn't there.>
<I was thankful for your skateboard, though.>
MAXIMUM
30
<It reminded me of my past, my heritage. And it reminded me of you, Yousef.>
<Unfortunately, some people were not so friendly.>
Hello! Excuse me, please.

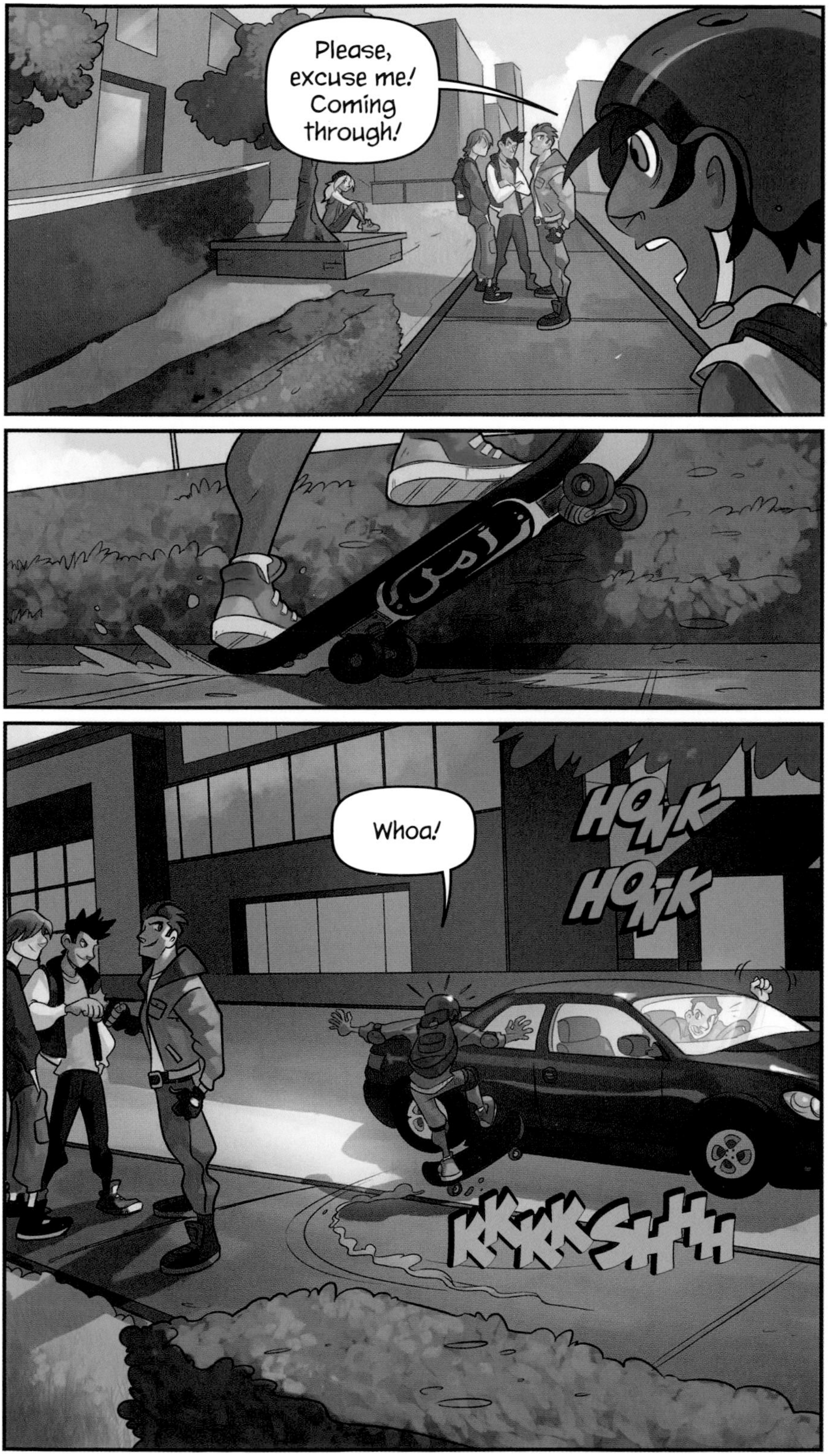
Please, excuse me! Coming through!
Whoa!
HONK HONK
KKKKSHHH

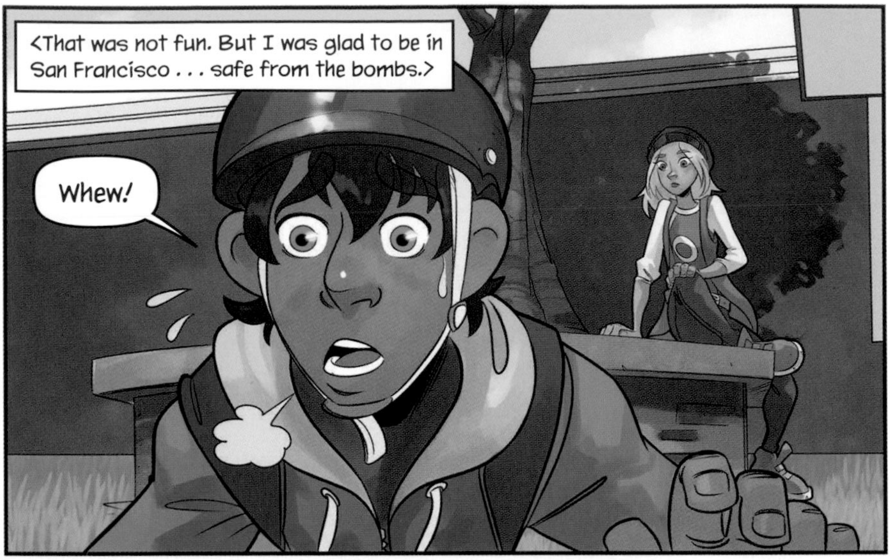
<That was not fun. But I was glad to be in San Francisco . . . safe from the bombs.>
Whew!

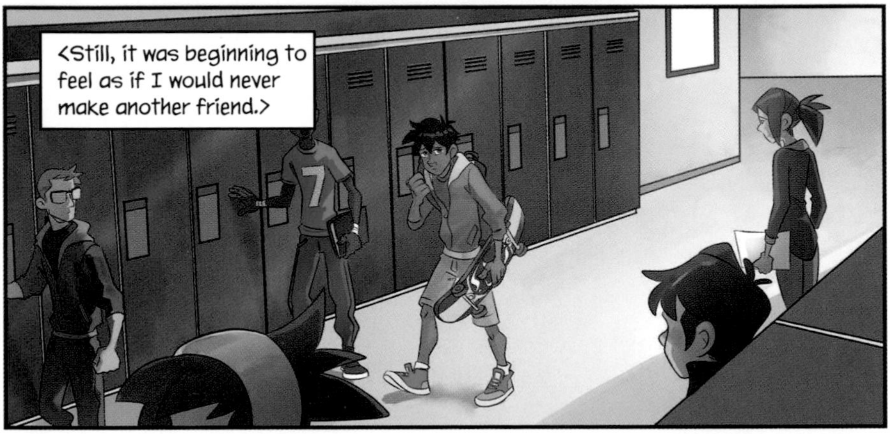
<Still, it was beginning to feel as if I would never make another friend.>

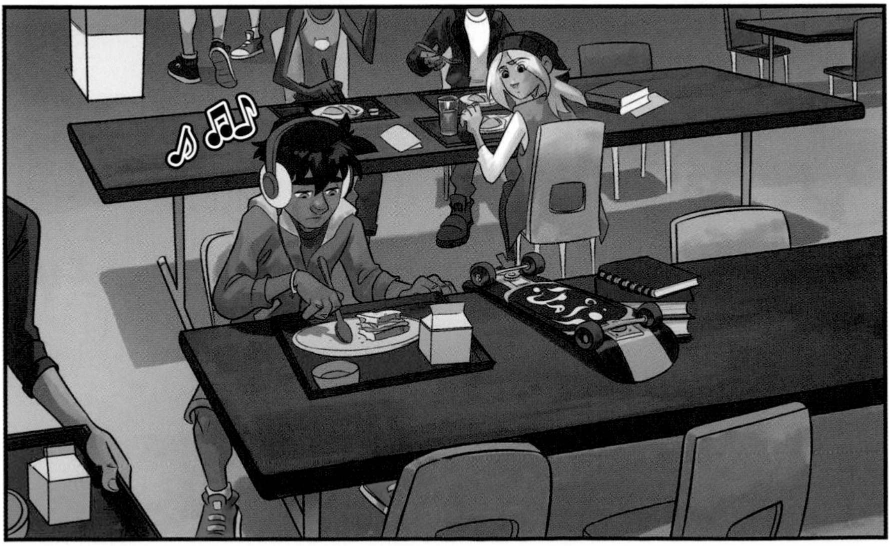

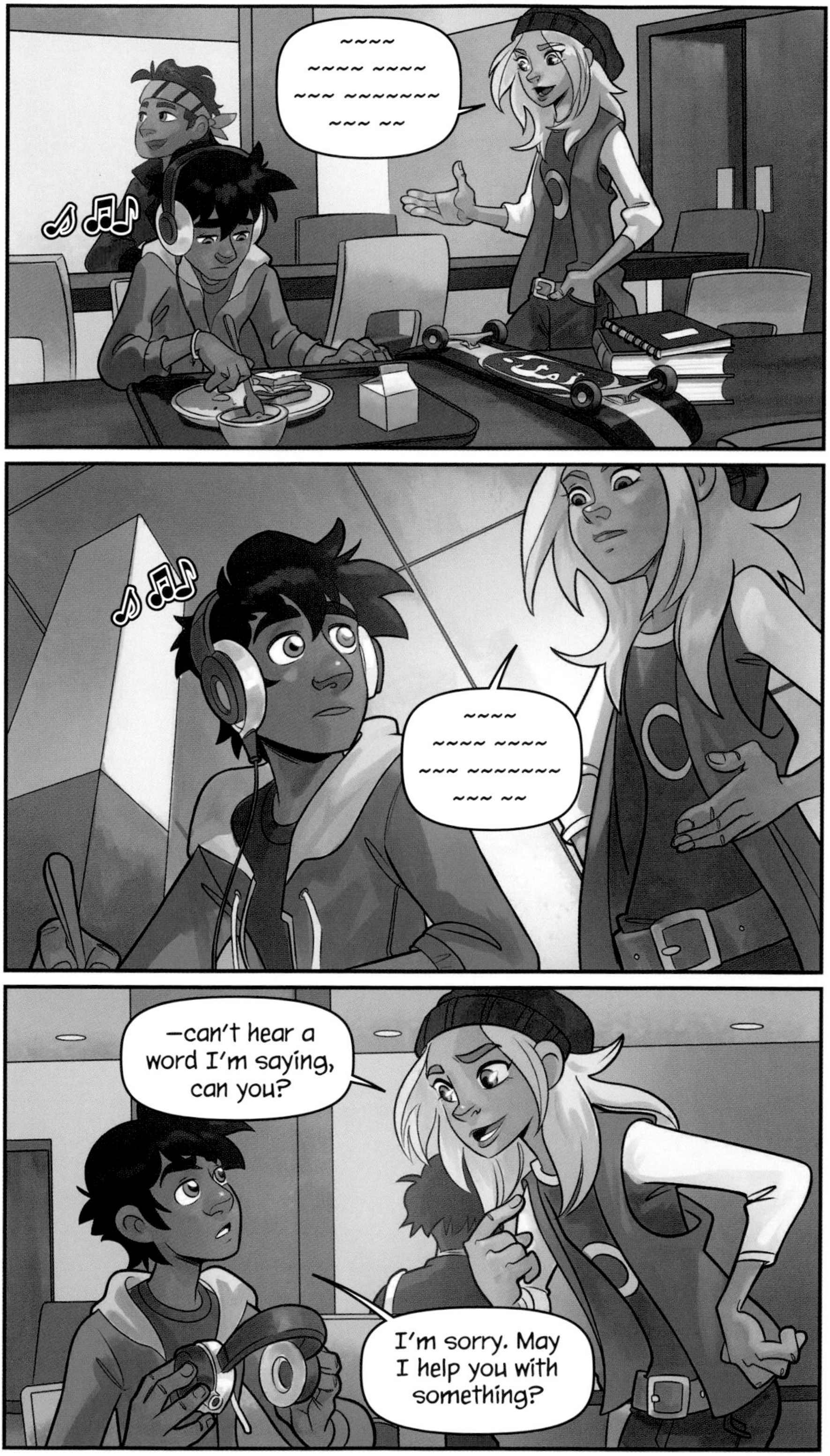
~~~~
~~~~ ~~~~
~~~ ~~~~~~~
~~~ ~~
~~~~
~~~~ ~~~~
~~~ ~~~~~~~
~~~ ~~
—can't hear a word I'm saying, can you?
I'm sorry. May I help you with something?

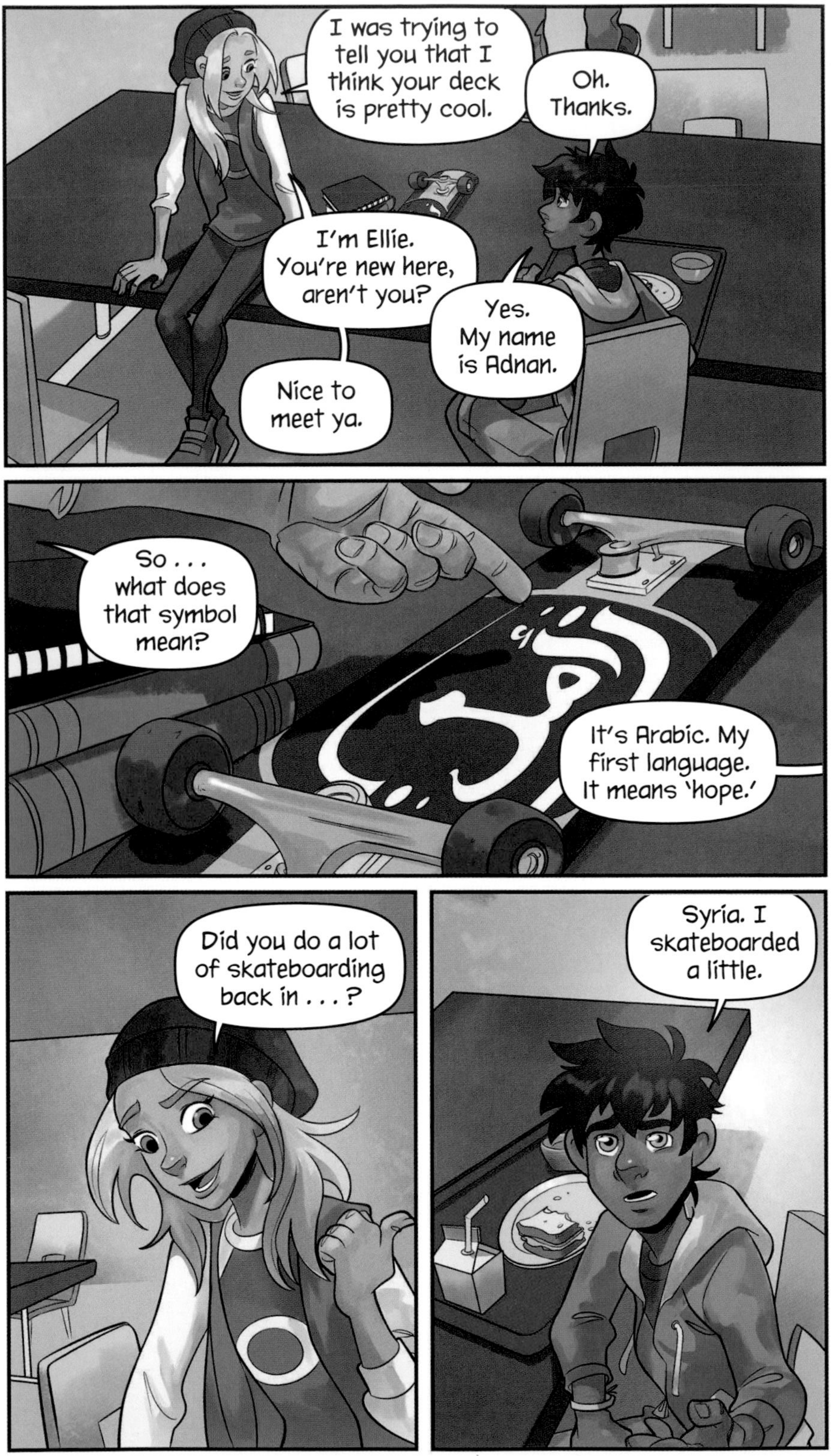
I was trying to tell you that I think your deck is pretty cool.
Oh. Thanks.
I'm Ellie. You're new here, aren't you?
Yes. My name is Adnan.
Nice to meet ya.
So . . . what does that symbol mean?
أمل
It's Arabic. My first language. It means 'hope.'
Did you do a lot of skateboarding back in . . . ?
Syria. I skateboarded a little.

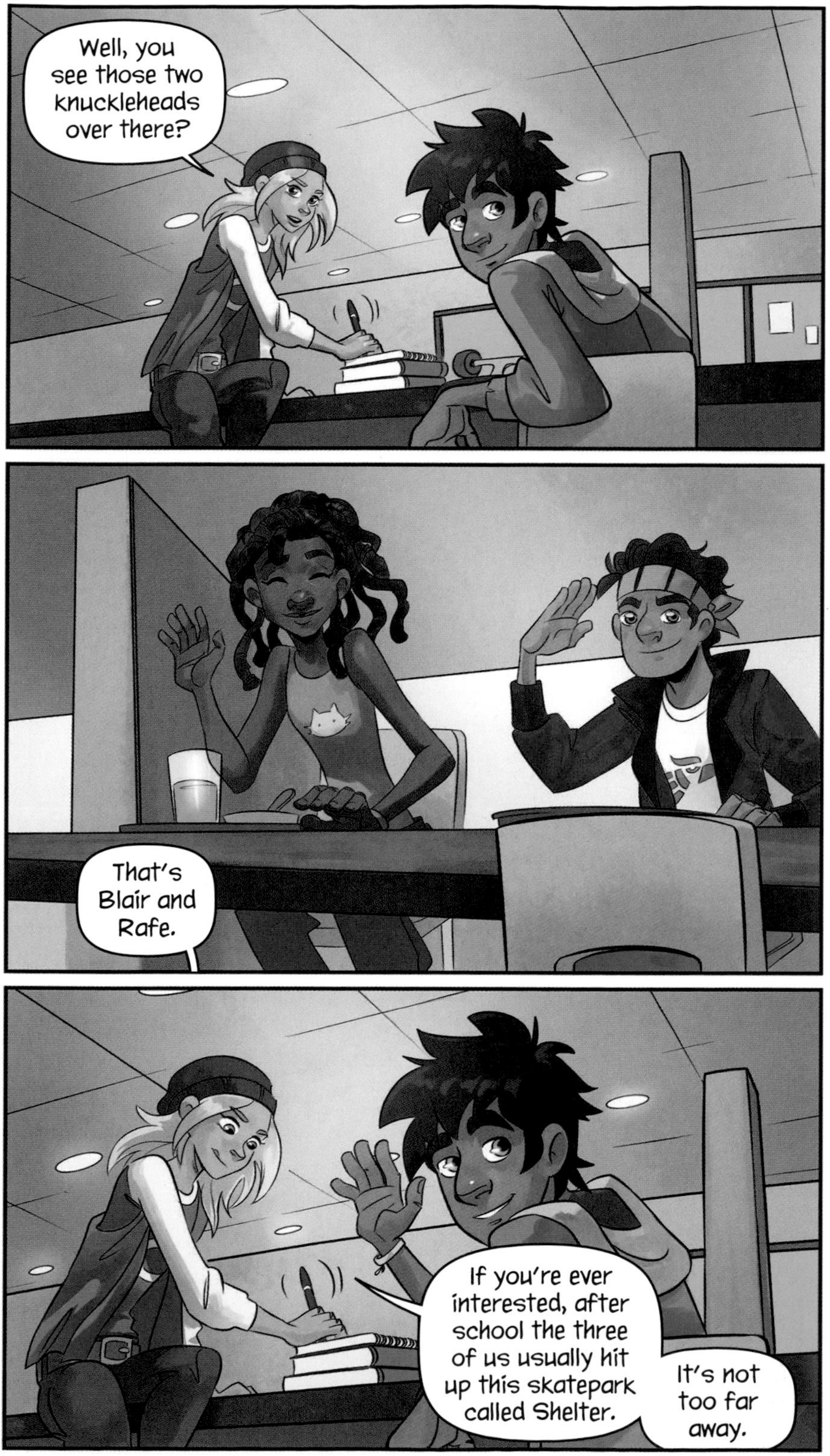
Well, you see those two knuckleheads over there?
That's Blair and Rafe.
If you're ever interested, after school the three of us usually hit up this skatepark called Shelter.
It's not too far away.

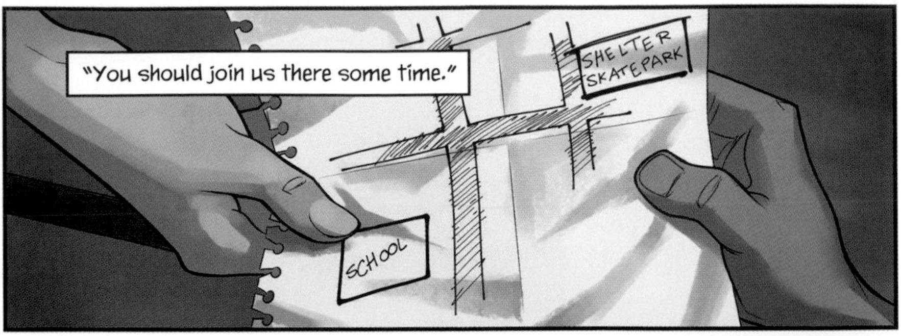
"You should join us there some time."
SHELTER SKATEPARK
SCHOOL

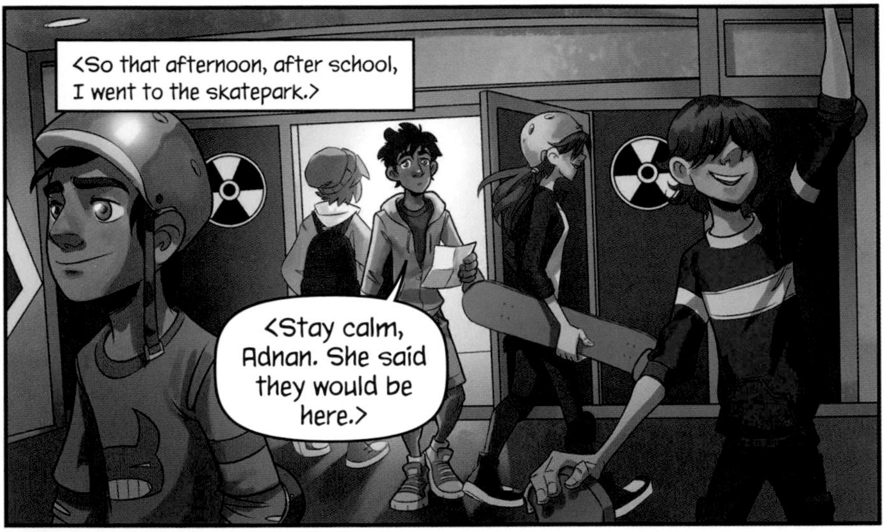
<So that afternoon, after school, I went to the skatepark.>
<Stay calm, Adnan. She said they would be here.>

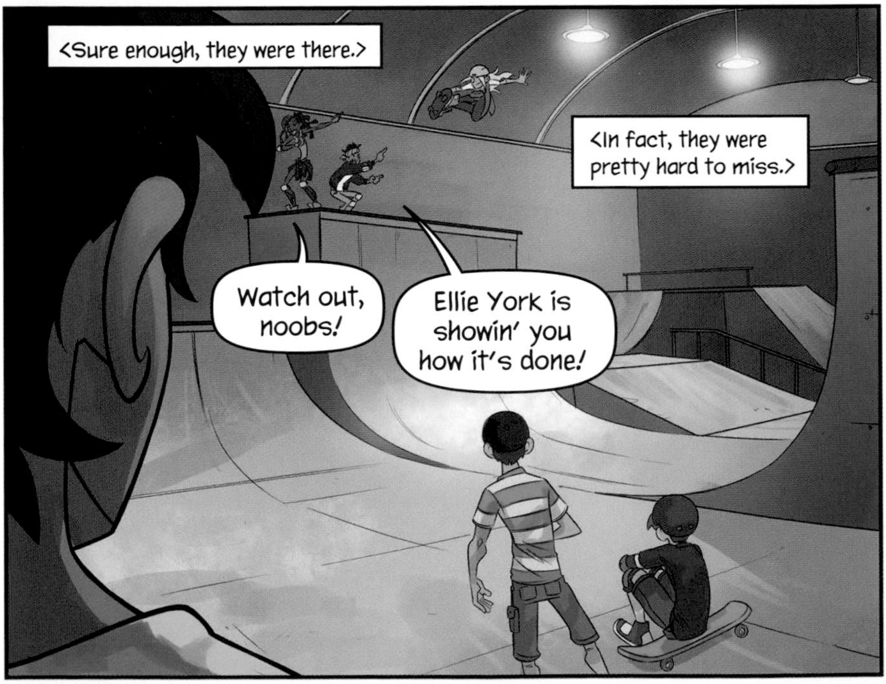
<Sure enough, they were there.>
<In fact, they were pretty hard to miss.>
Watch out, noobs!
Ellie York is showin' you how it's done!

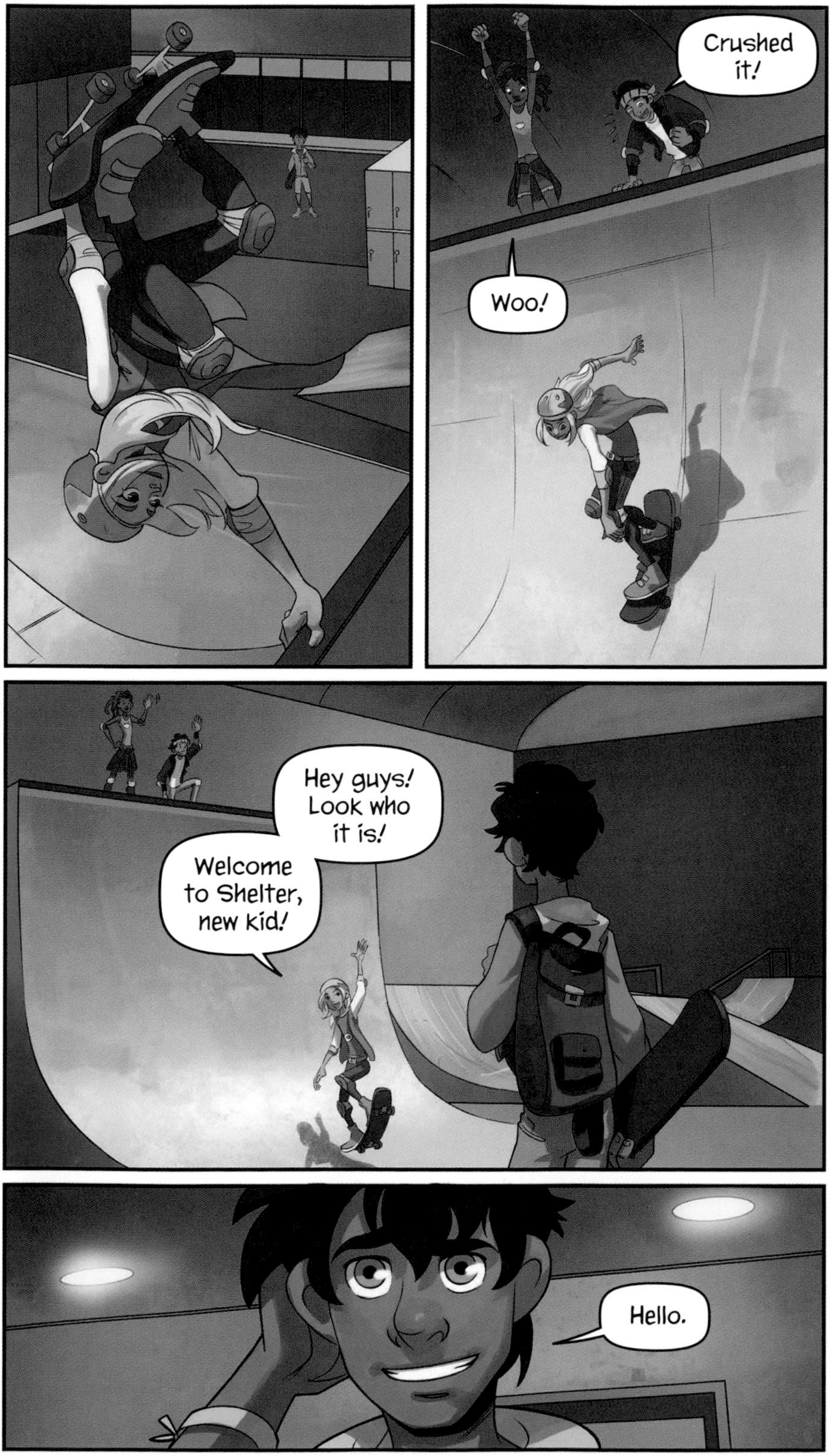
Crushed it!
Woo!
Hey guys! Look who it is!
Welcome to Shelter, new kid!
Hello.

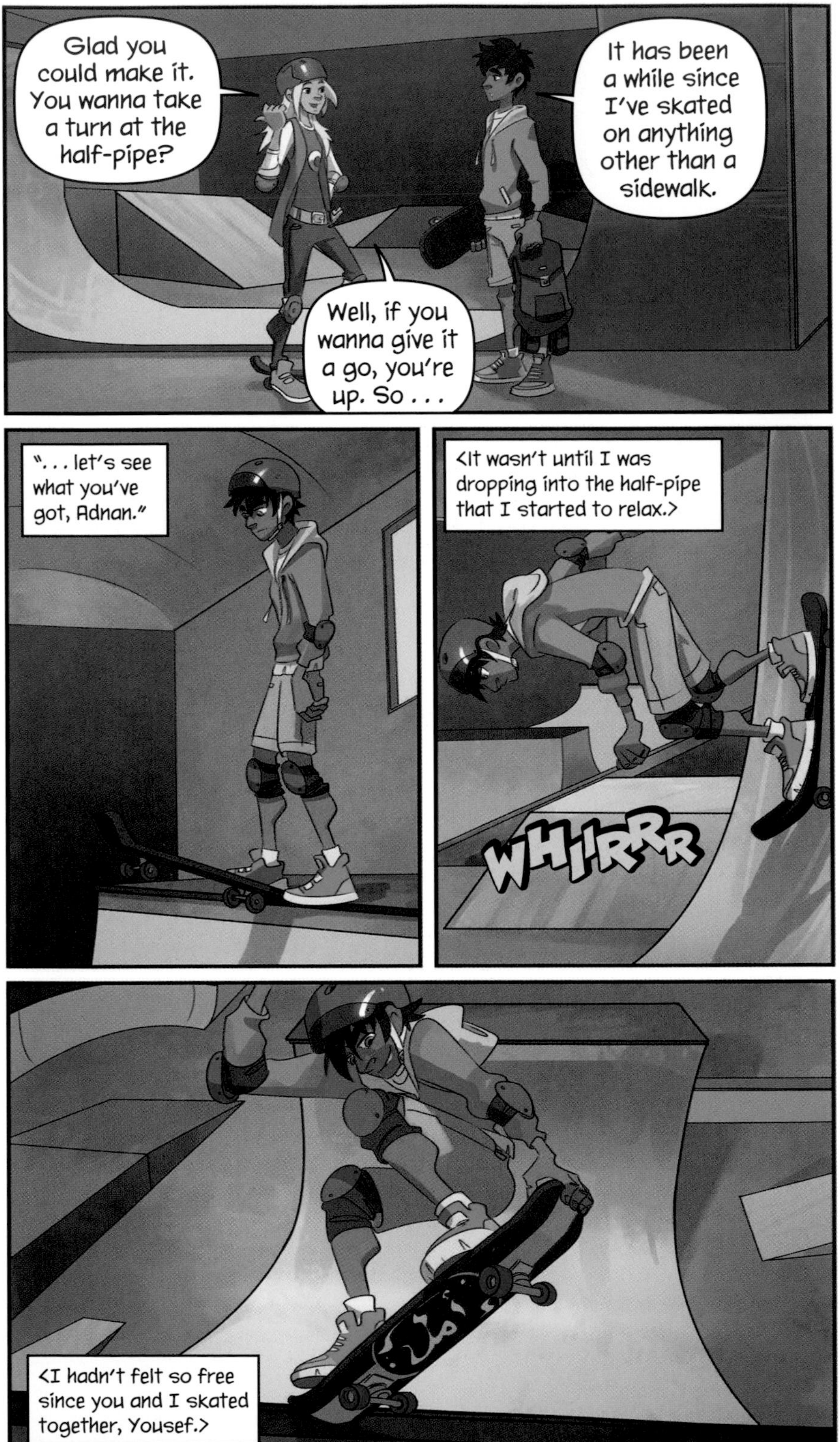
Glad you could make it. You wanna take a turn at the half-pipe?
It has been a while since I've skated on anything other than a sidewalk.
Well, if you wanna give it a go, you're up. So . . .
". . . let's see what you've got, Adnan."
<It wasn't until I was dropping into the half-pipe that I started to relax.>
WHIRRR
<I hadn't felt so free since you and I skated together, Yousef.>

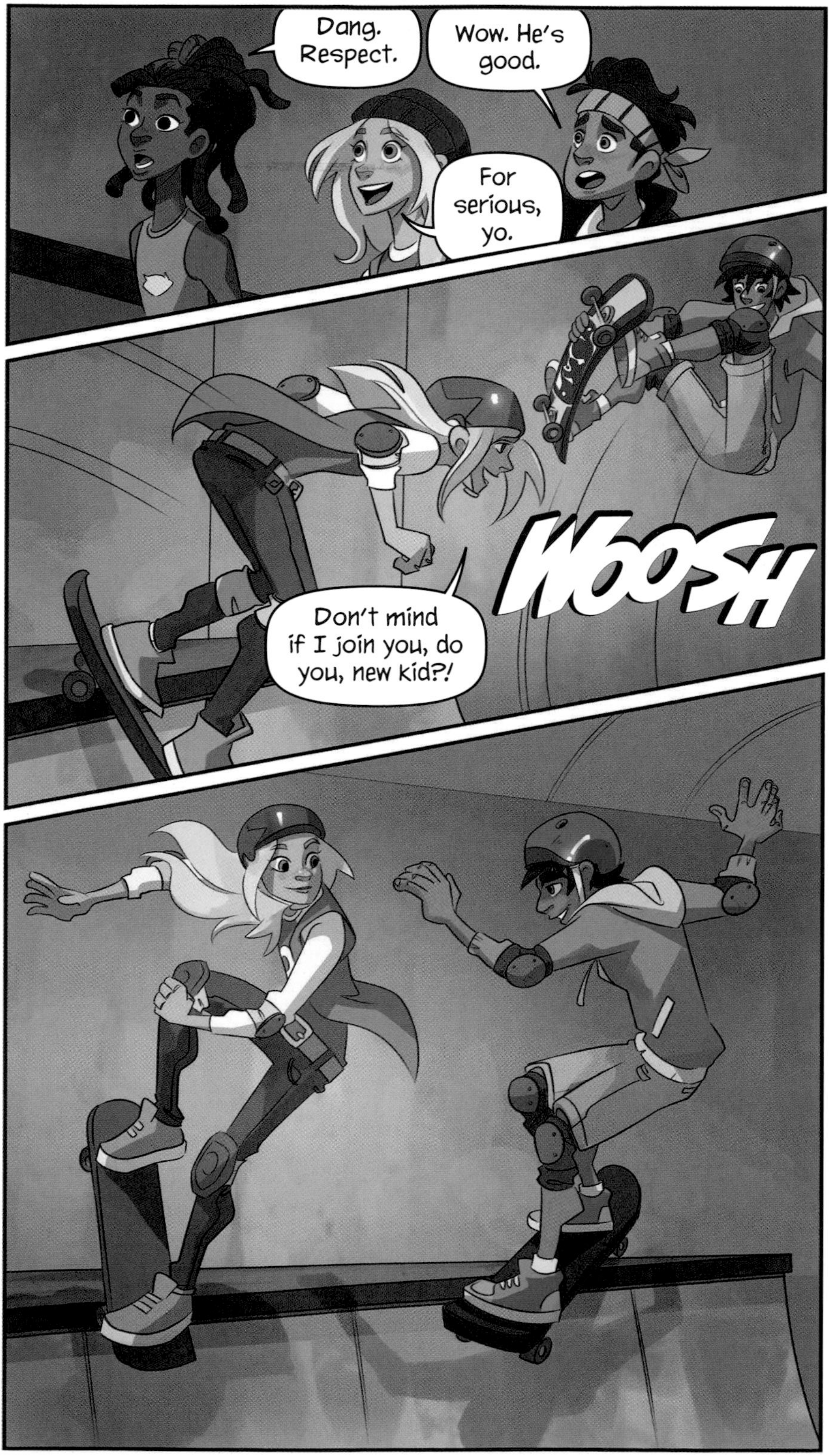
Dang. Respect.
Wow. He's good.
For serious, yo.
WOOSH
Don't mind if I join you, do you, new kid?!

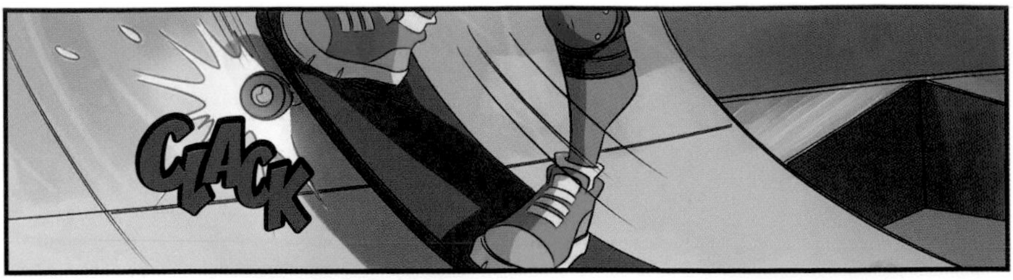
CLACK
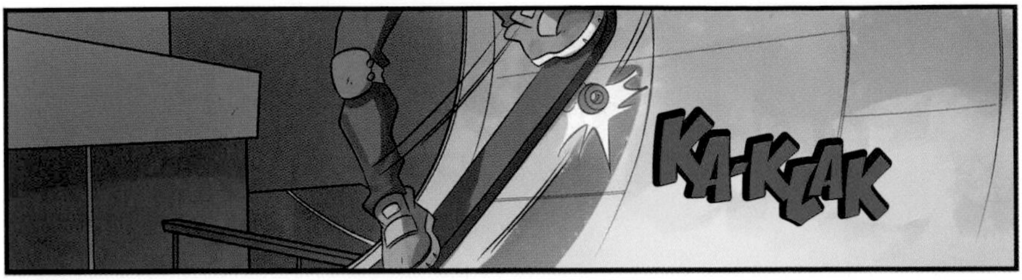
KA-KLAK
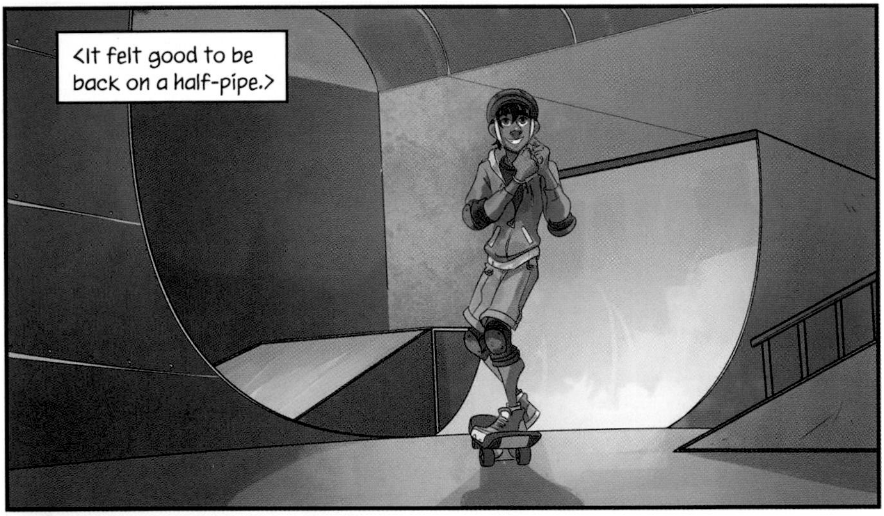
<It felt good to be back on a half-pipe.>
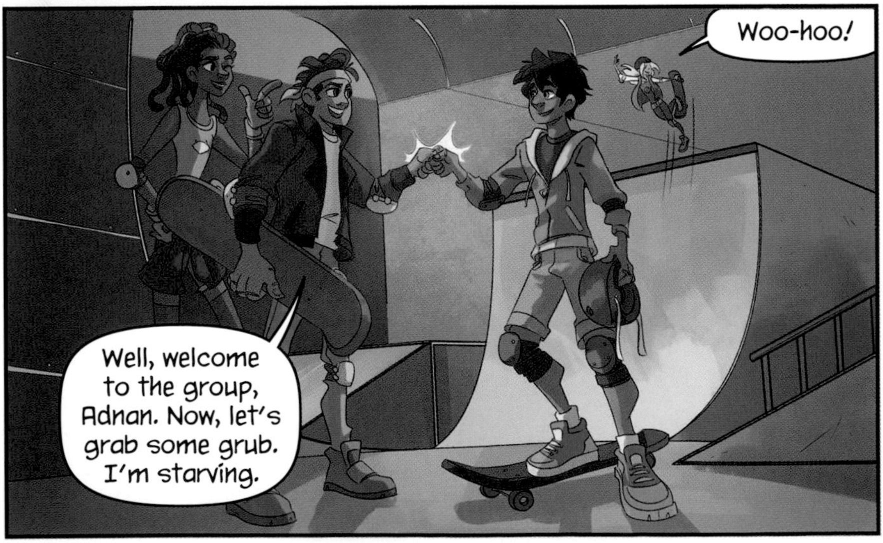
Woo-hoo!
Well, welcome to the group, Adnan. Now, let's grab some grub. I'm starving.

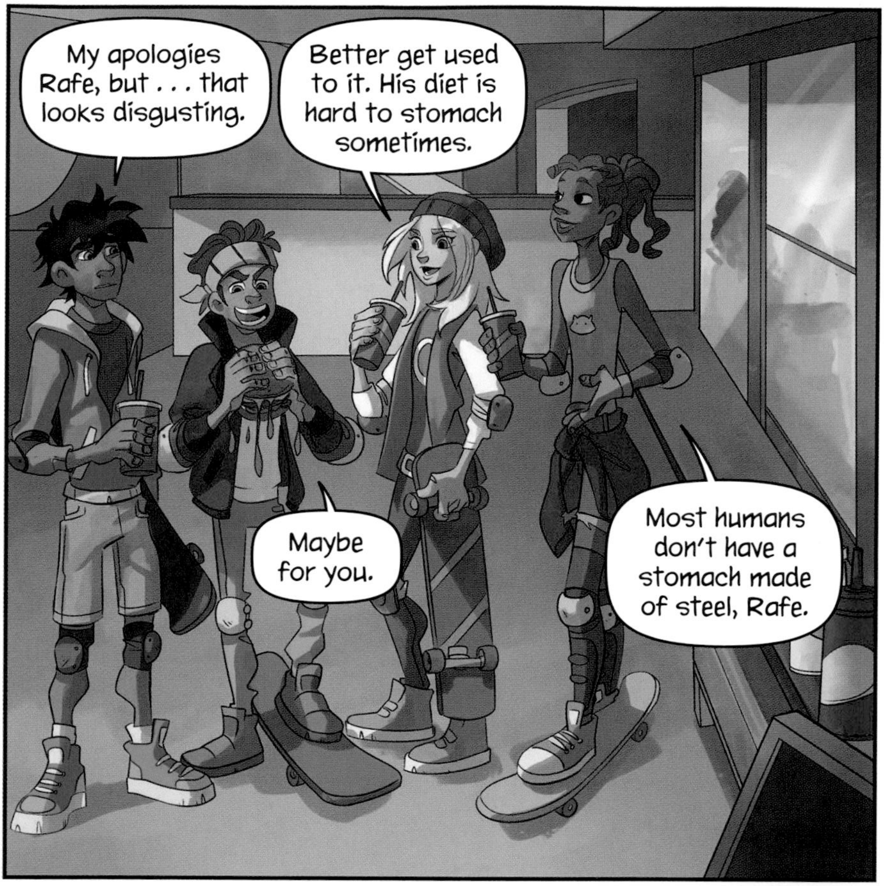
My apologies Rafe, but . . . that looks disgusting.
Better get used to it. His diet is hard to stomach sometimes.
Maybe for you.
Most humans don't have a stomach made of steel, Rafe.

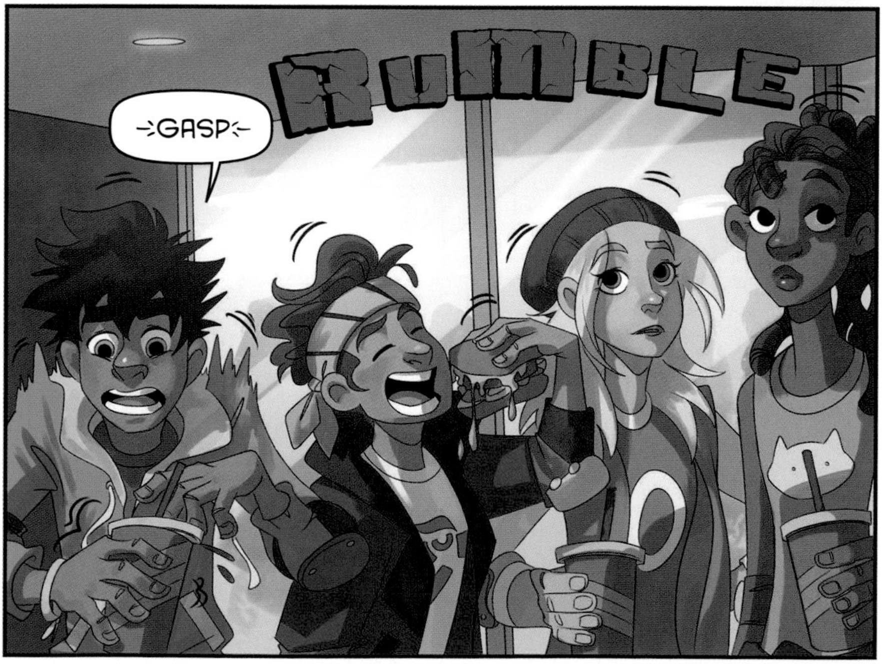
RUMBLE
GASP

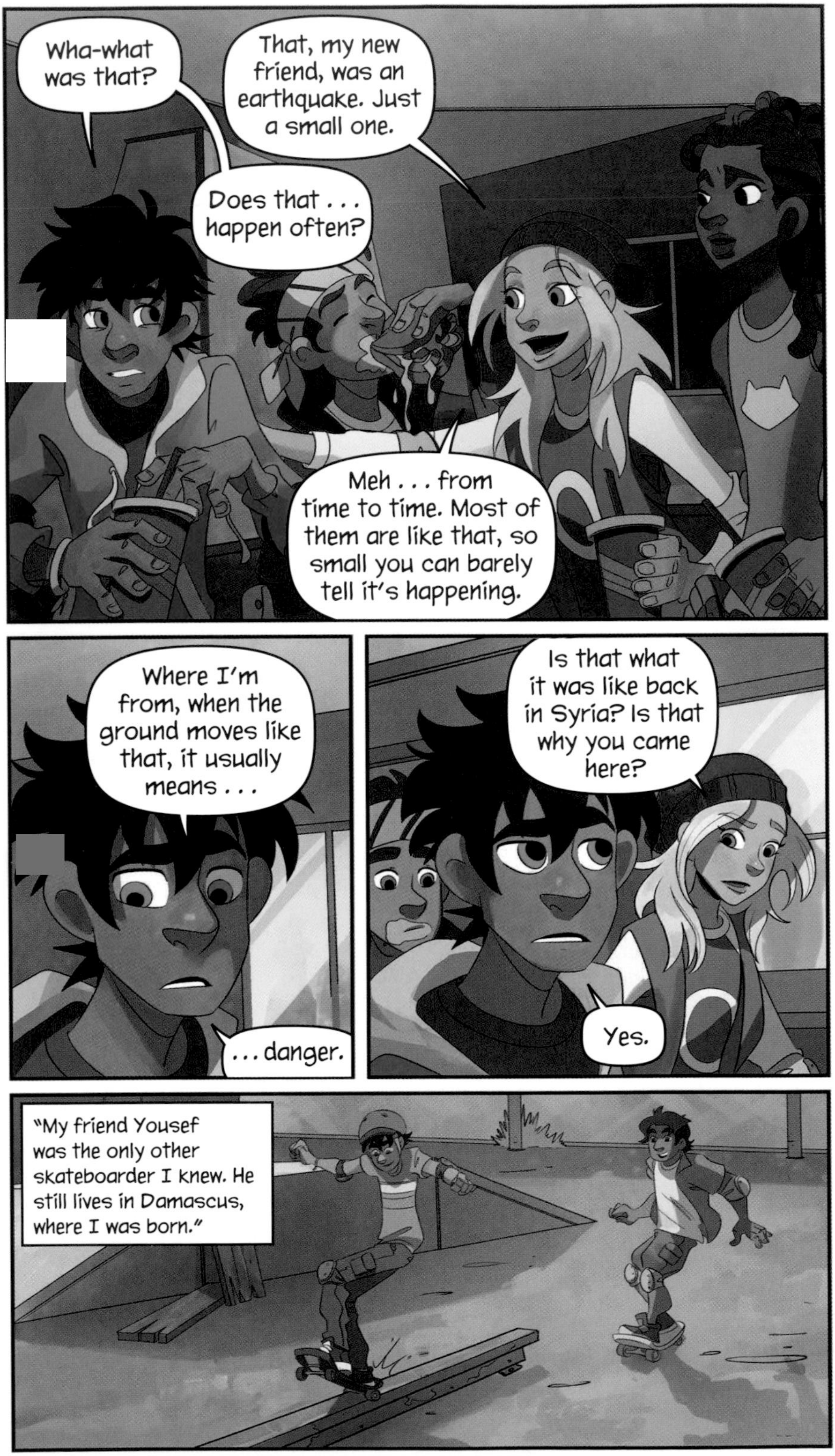
Wha-what was that?
That, my new friend, was an earthquake. Just a small one.
Does that . . . happen often?
Meh . . . from time to time. Most of them are like that, so small you can barely tell it's happening.
Where I'm from, when the ground moves like that, it usually means . . .
. . . danger.
Is that what it was like back in Syria? Is that why you came here?
Yes.
"My friend Yousef was the only other skateboarder I knew. He still lives in Damascus, where I was born."

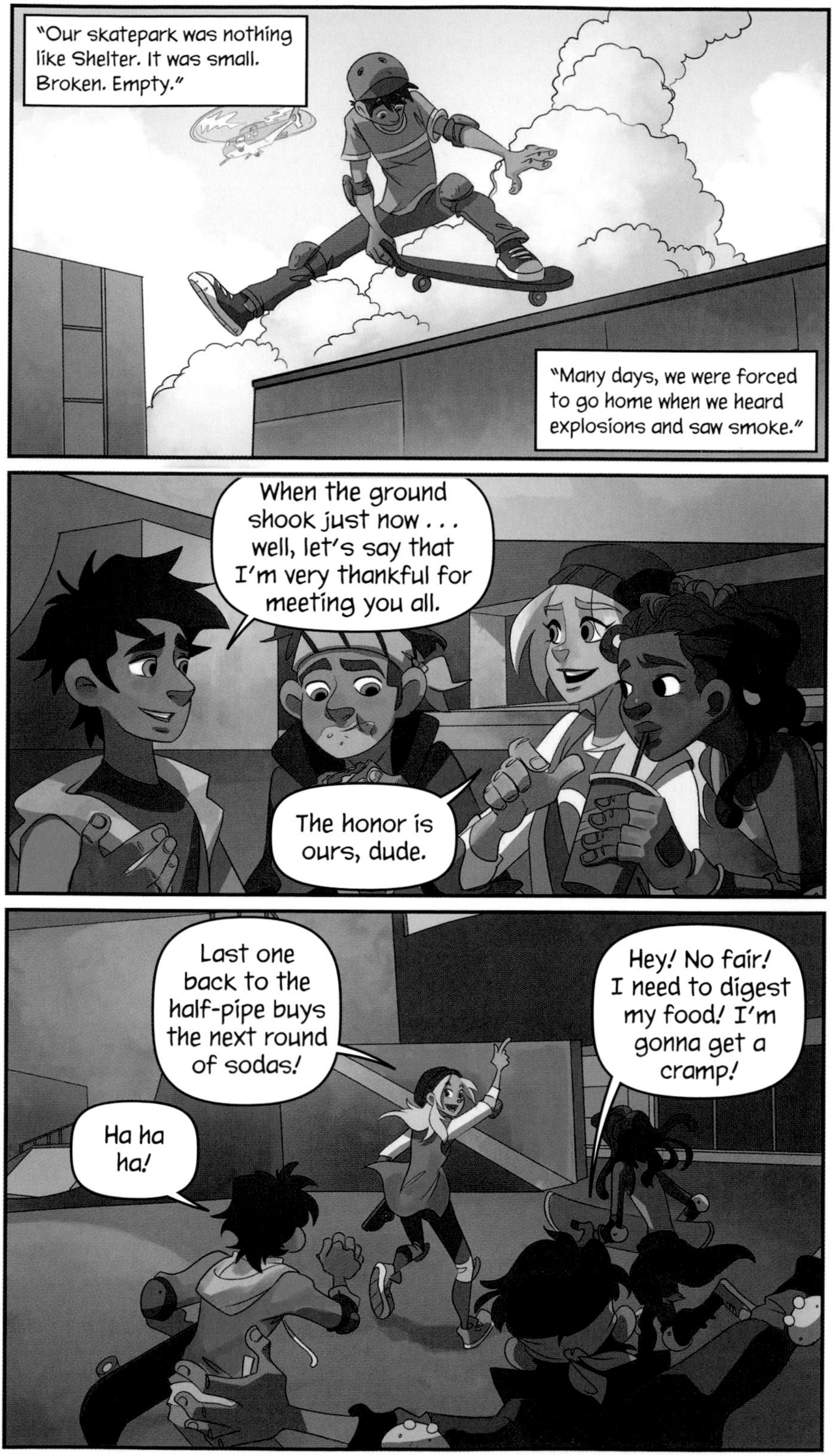
"Our skatepark was nothing like Shelter. It was small. Broken. Empty."
"Many days, we were forced to go home when we heard explosions and saw smoke."
When the ground shook just now . . . well, let's say that I'm very thankful for meeting you all.
The honor is ours, dude.
Last one back to the half-pipe buys the next round of sodas!
Hey! No fair! I need to digest my food! I'm gonna get a cramp!
Ha ha ha!

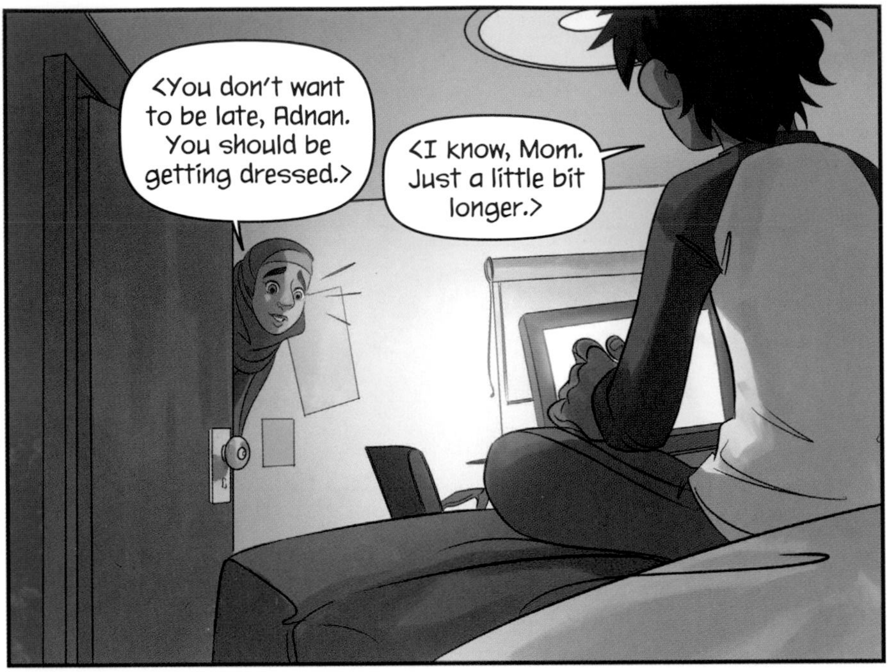
<You don't want to be late, Adnan. You should be getting dressed.>
<I know, Mom. Just a little bit longer.>

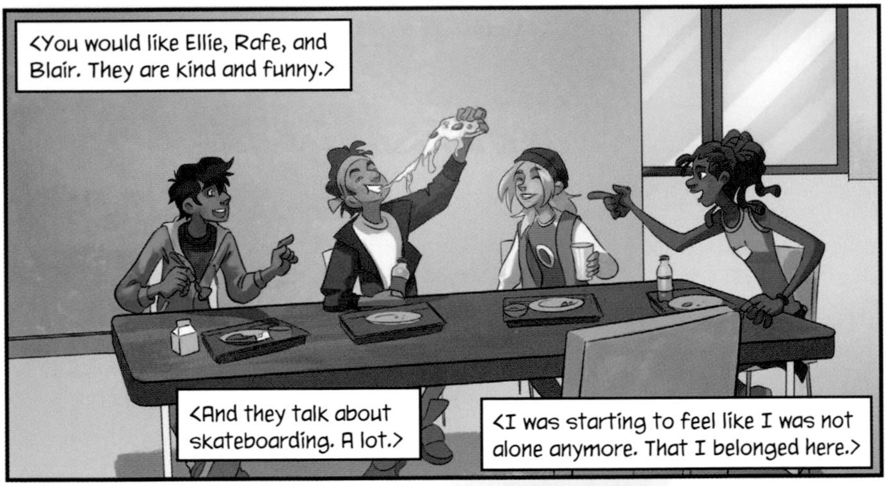
<You would like Ellie, Rafe, and Blair. They are kind and funny.>
<And they talk about skateboarding. A lot.>
<I was starting to feel like I was not alone anymore. That I belonged here.>

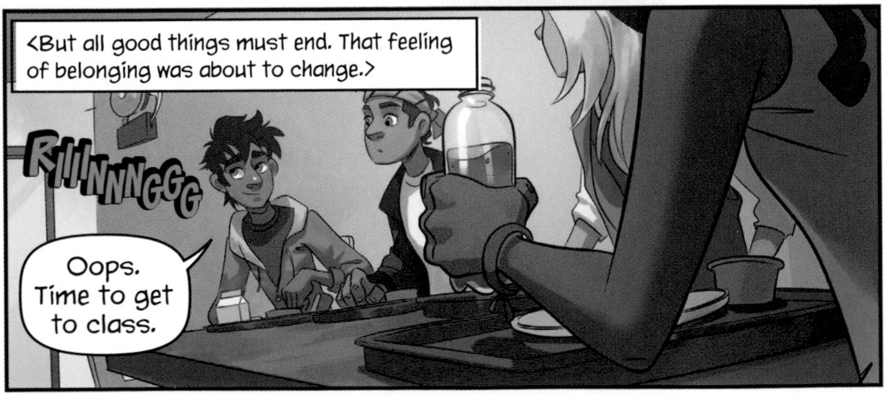
<But all good things must end. That feeling of belonging was about to change.>
RIIINNNGGG
Oops. Time to get to class.

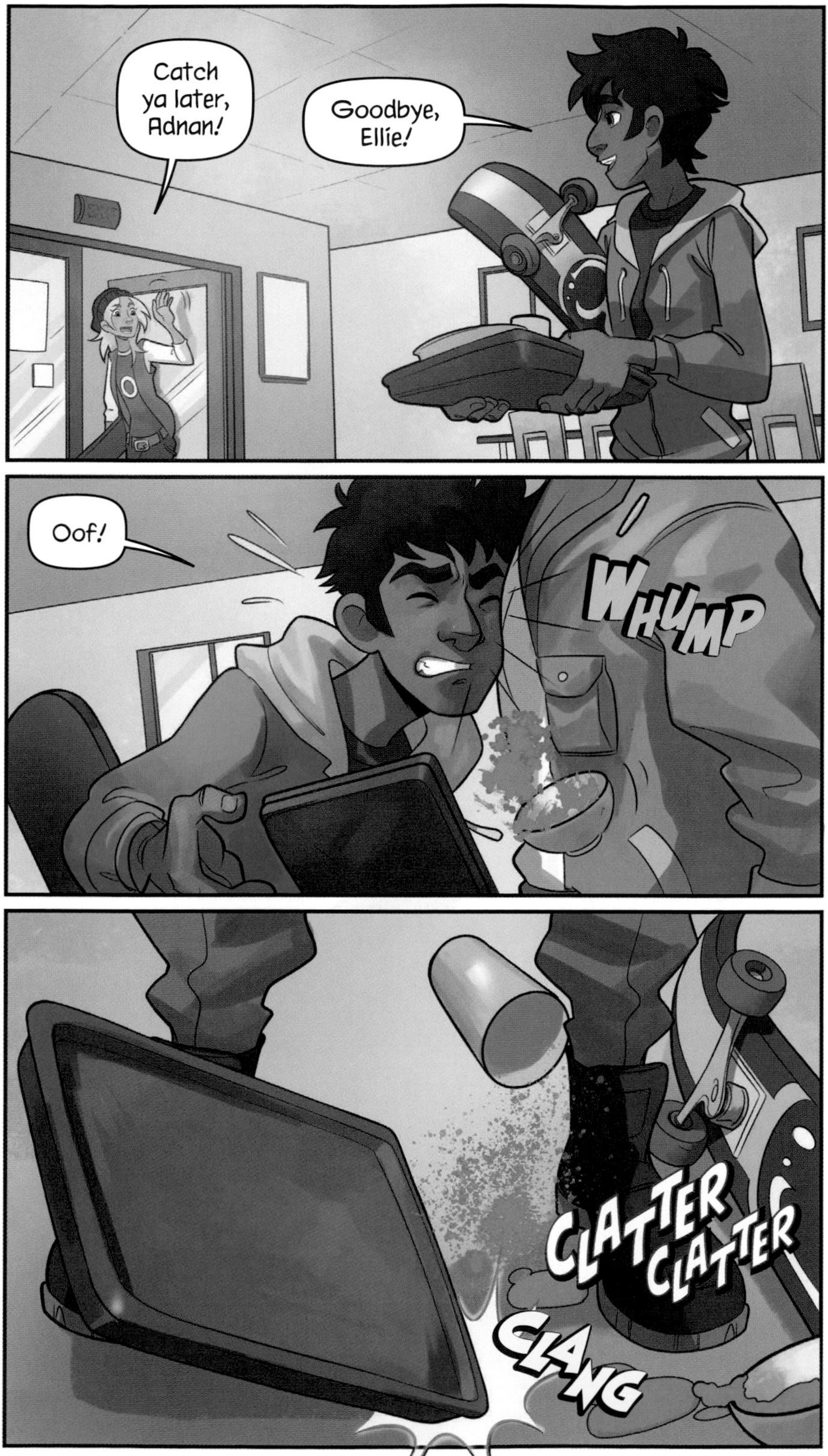
Catch ya later, Adnan!
Goodbye, Ellie!
Oof!
WHUMP
CLATTER CLATTER
CLANG

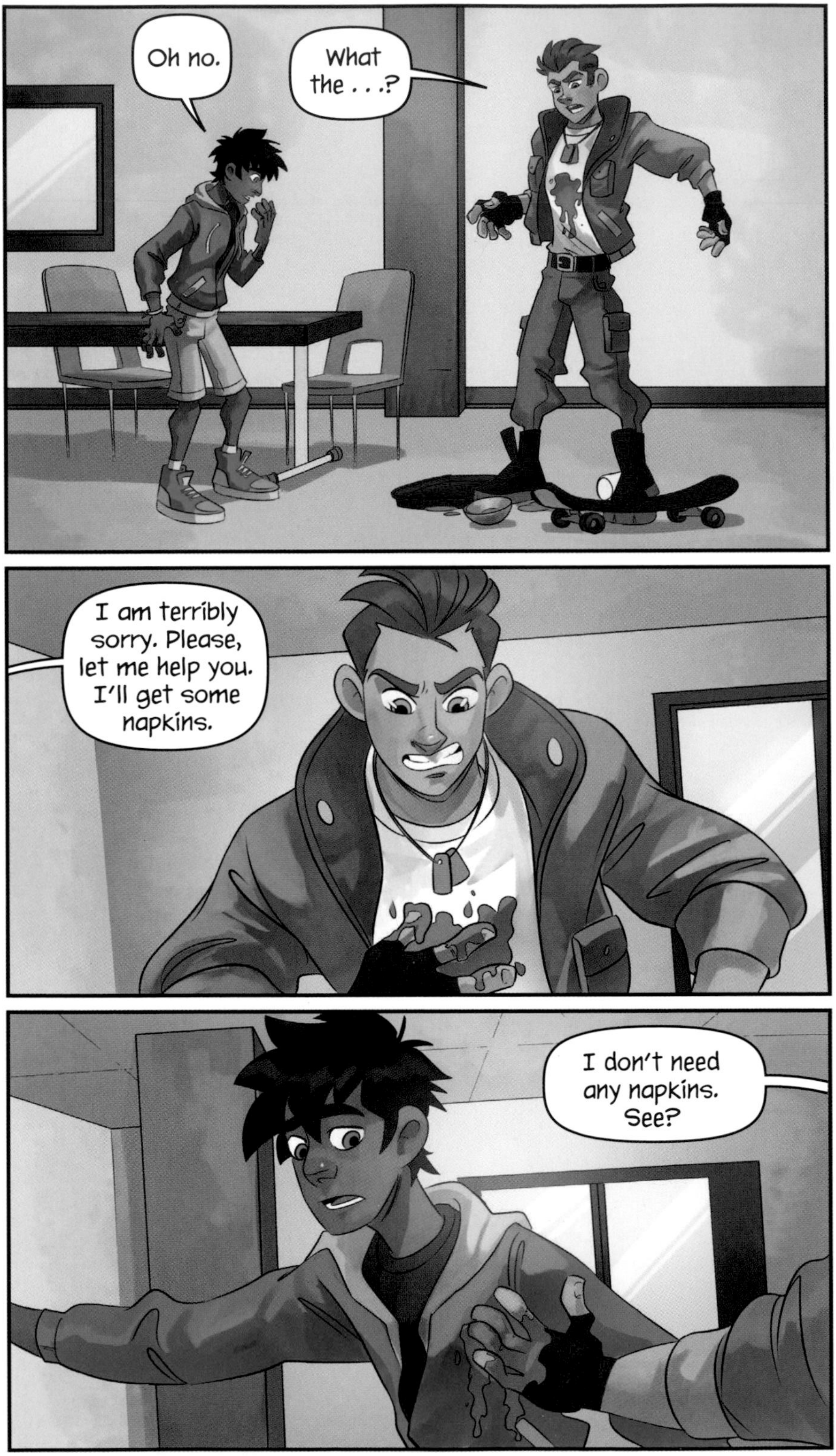
Oh no.
What the . . .?
I am terribly sorry. Please, let me help you. I'll get some napkins.
I don't need any napkins. See?

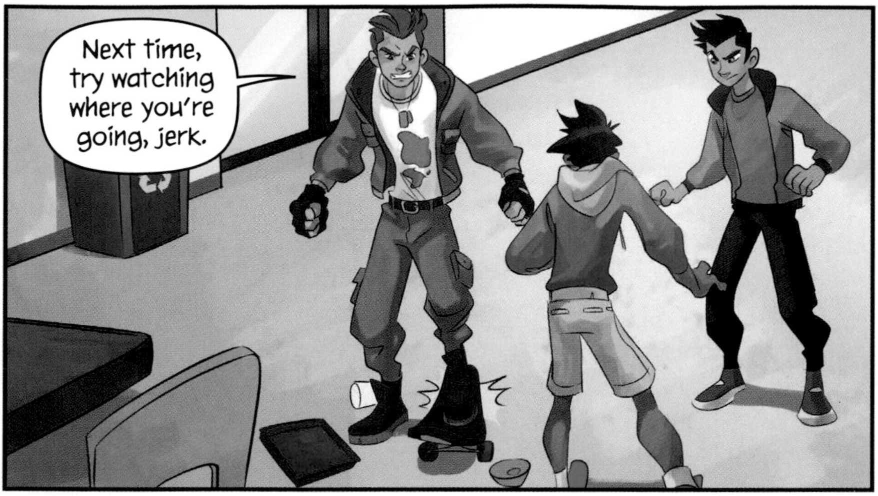
Next time, try watching where you're going, jerk.

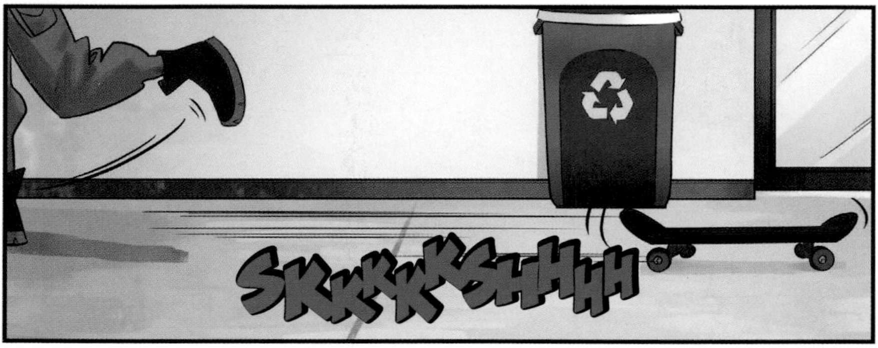
SKKKKSHHHH

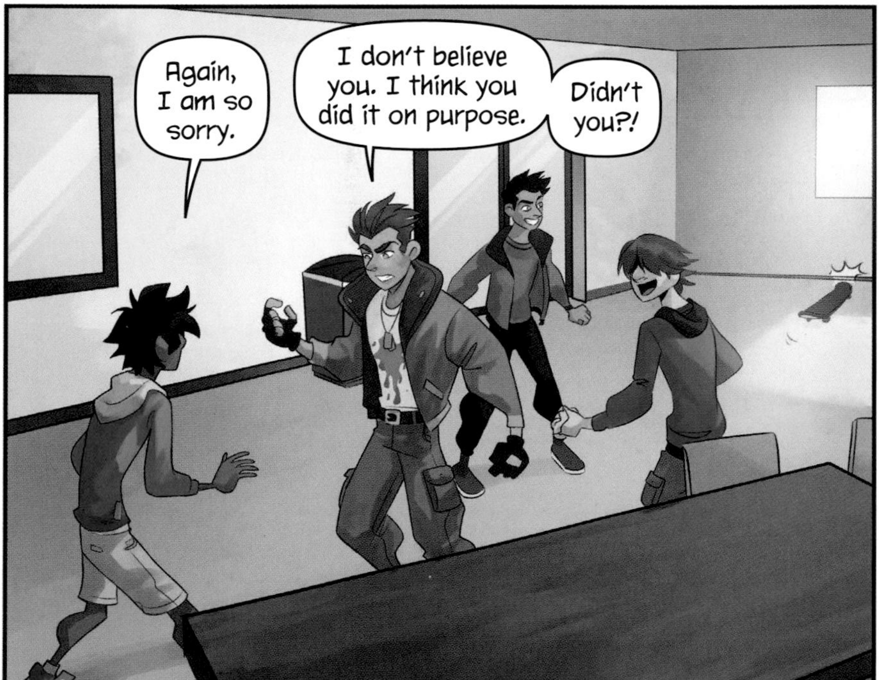
Again, I am so sorry.
I don't believe you. I think you did it on purpose.
Didn't you?!

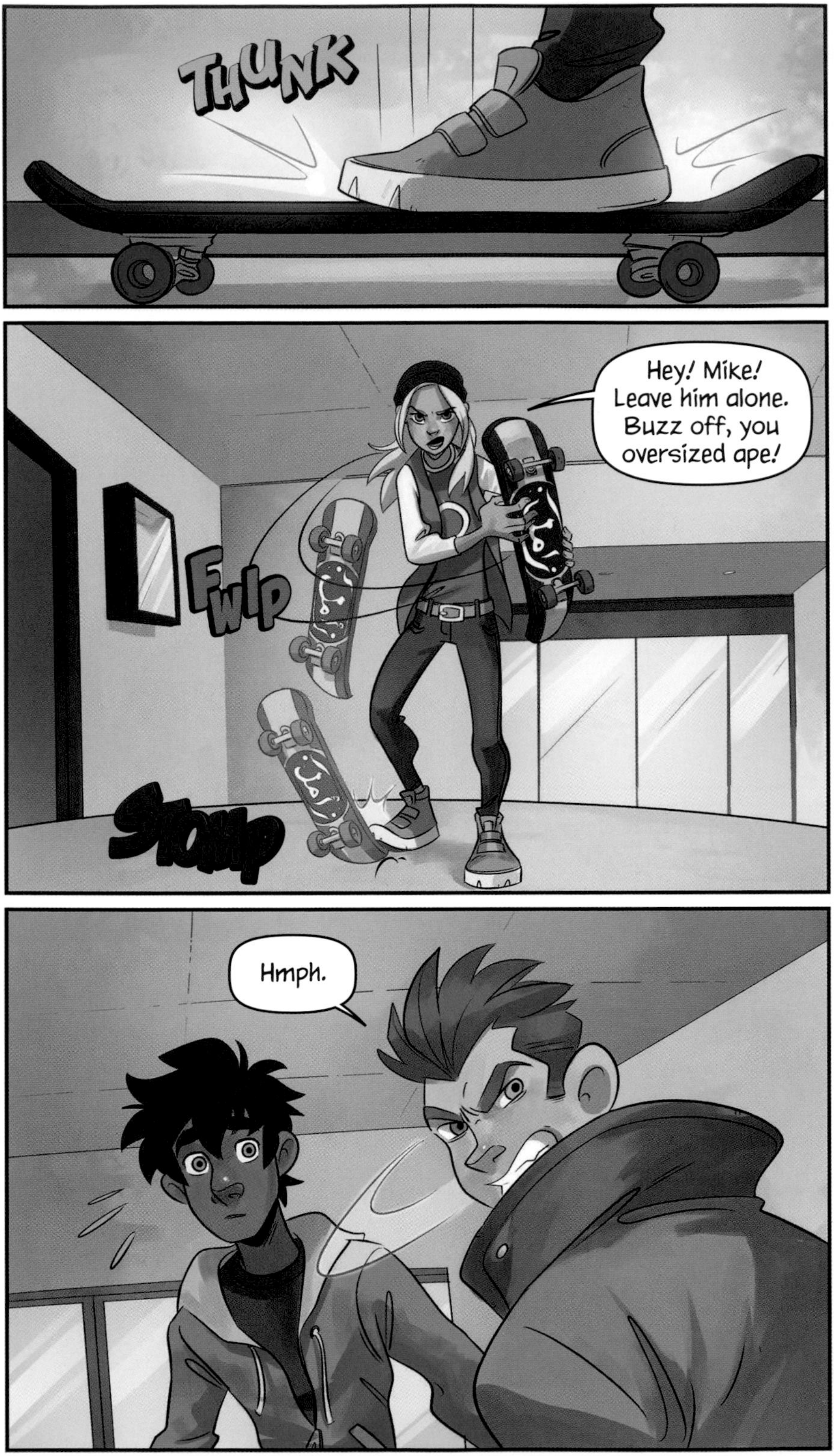
THUNK
Hey! Mike! Leave him alone. Buzz off, you oversized ape!
FWIP
STOMP
Hmph.

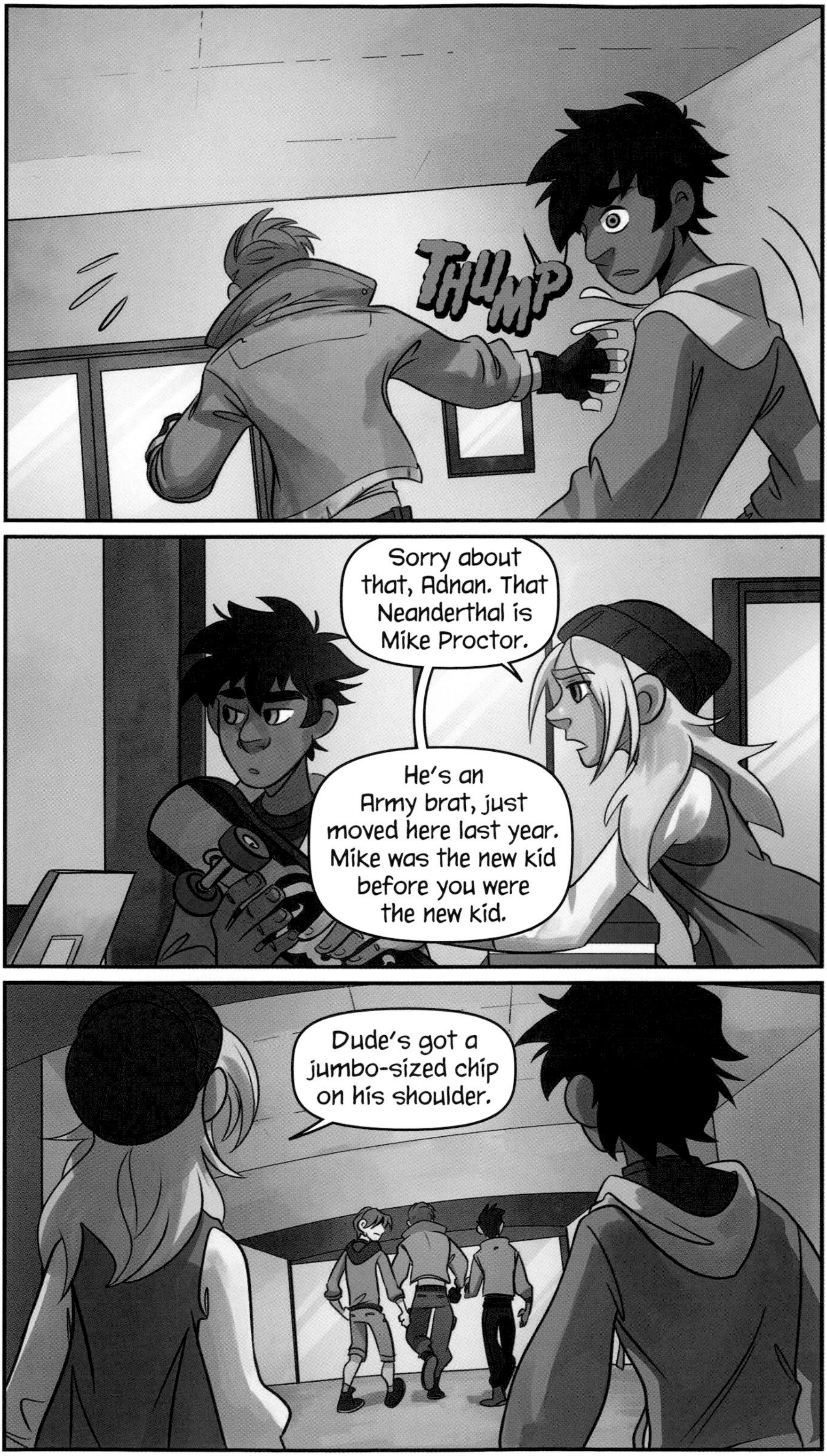
THUMP
Sorry about that, Adnan. That Neanderthal is Mike Proctor.
He's an Army brat, just moved here last year. Mike was the new kid before you were the new kid.
Dude's got a jumbo-sized chip on his shoulder.

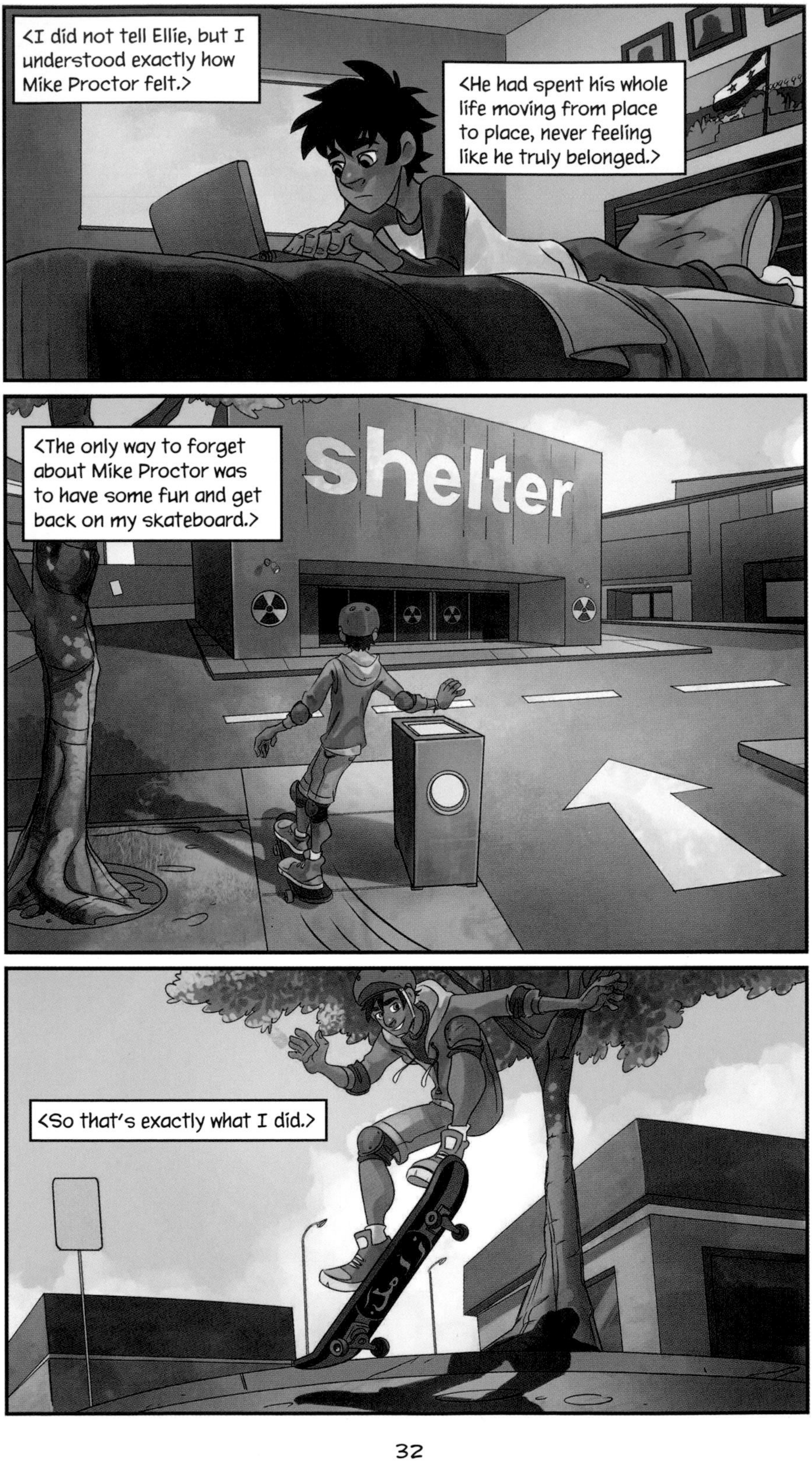
<I did not tell Ellie, but I understood exactly how Mike Proctor felt.>
<He had spent his whole life moving from place to place, never feeling like he truly belonged.>
<The only way to forget about Mike Proctor was to have some fun and get back on my skateboard.>
Shelter
<So that's exactly what I did.>

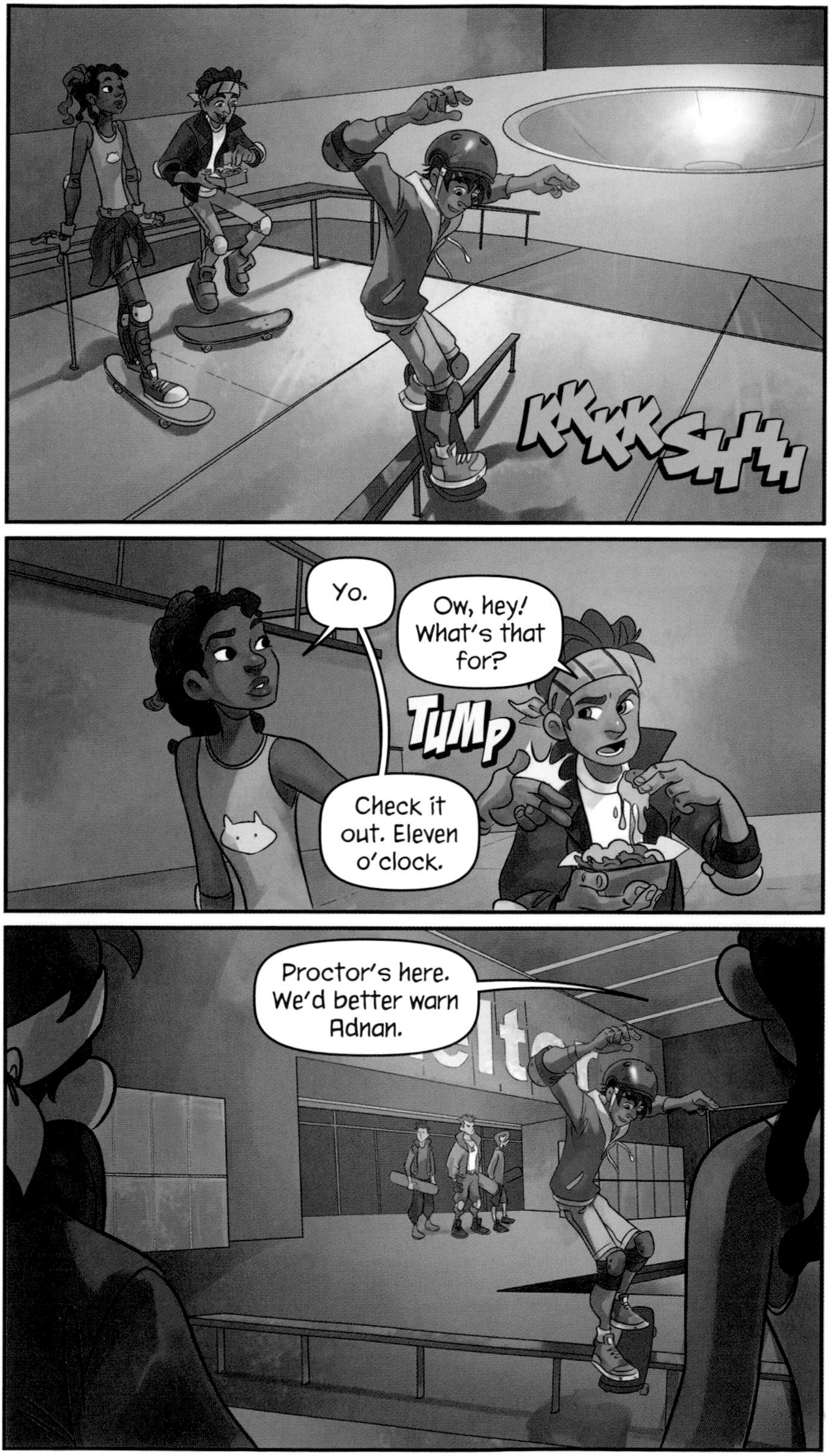
KKKKSHHH
Yo.
Ow, hey! What's that for?
TUMP
Check it out. Eleven o'clock.
Proctor's here. We'd better warn Adnan.

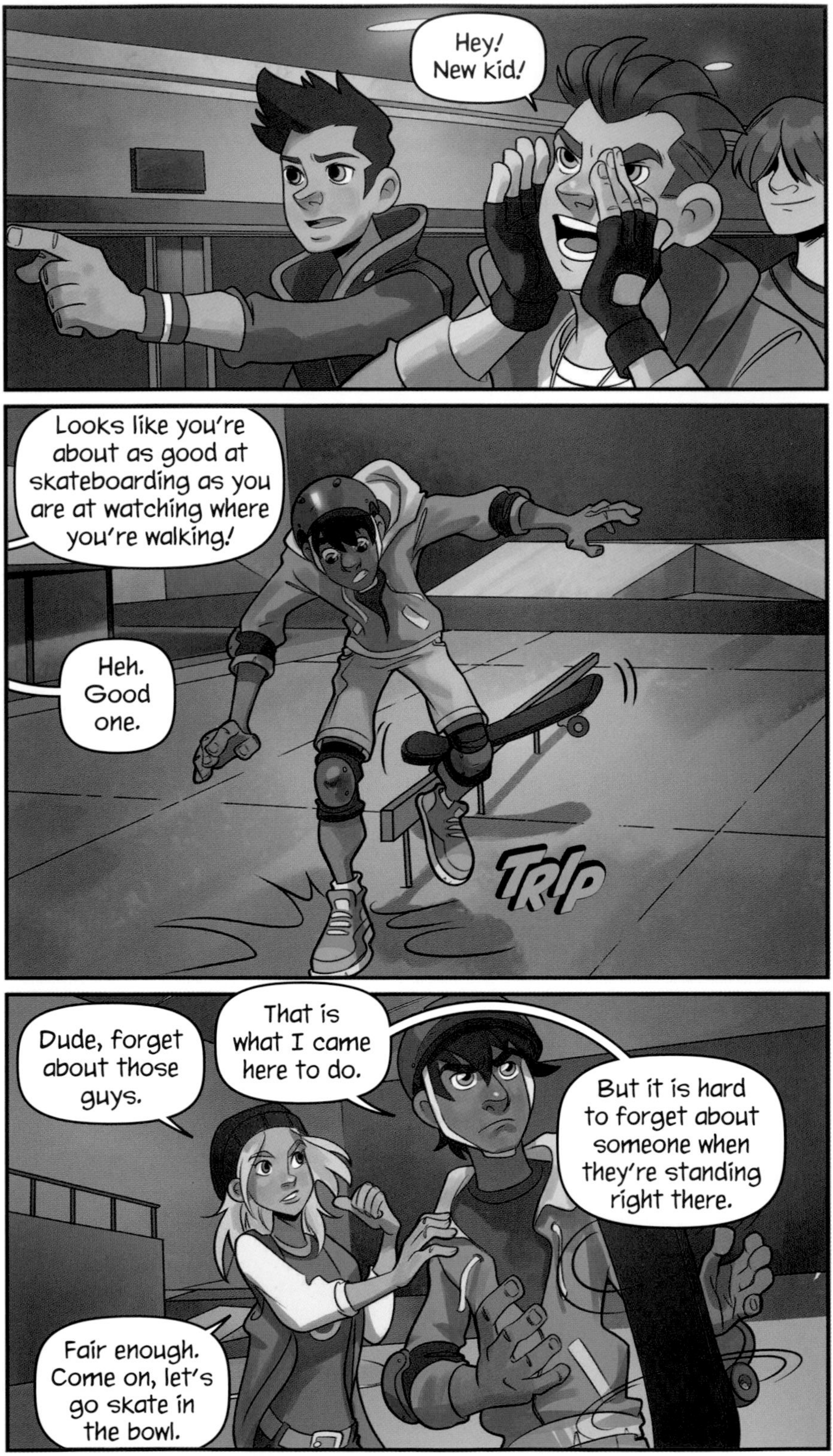
Hey! New kid!
Looks like you're about as good at skateboarding as you are at watching where you're walking!
Heh. Good one.
TRIP
Dude, forget about those guys.
That is what I came here to do.
But it is hard to forget about someone when they're standing right there.
Fair enough. Come on, let's go skate in the bowl.

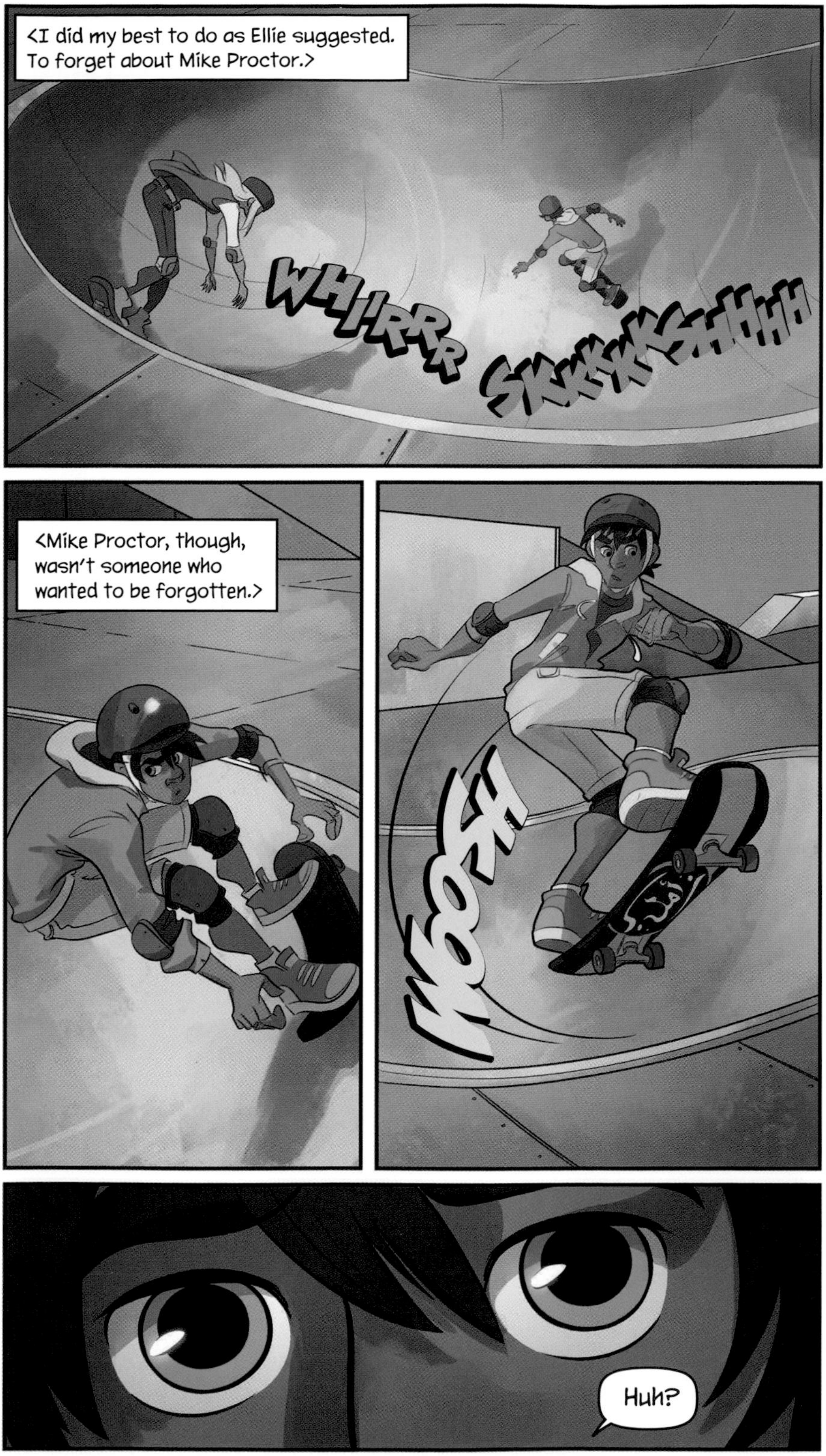
<I did my best to do as Ellie suggested. To forget about Mike Proctor.>
WHIRRR
SKKKKSHHHHH
<Mike Proctor, though, wasn't someone who wanted to be forgotten.>
WOOSH
Huh?

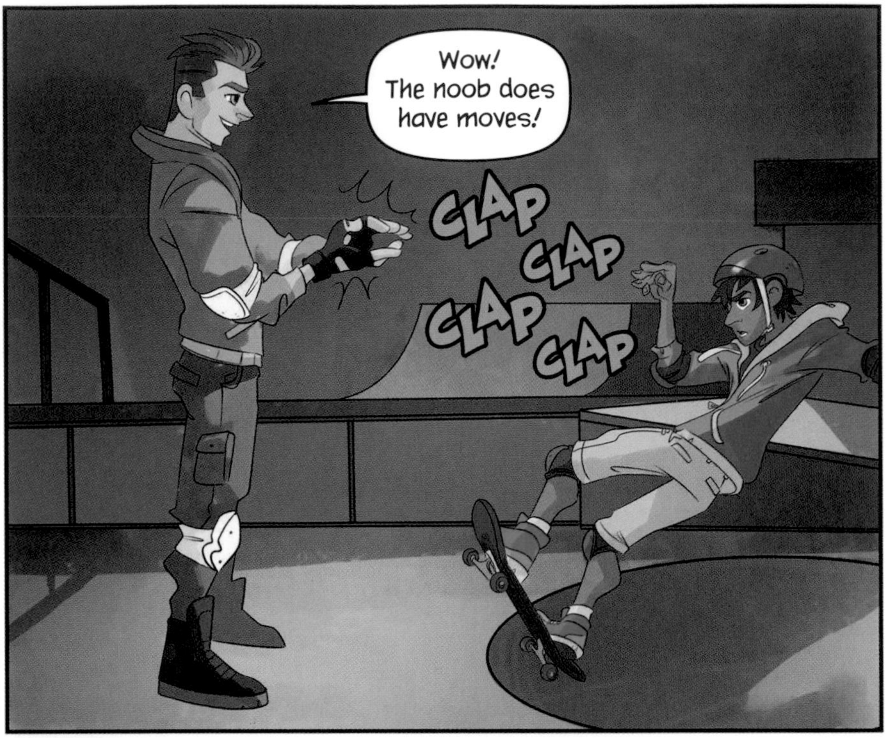
Wow! The noob does have moves!
CLAP CLAP CLAP CLAP

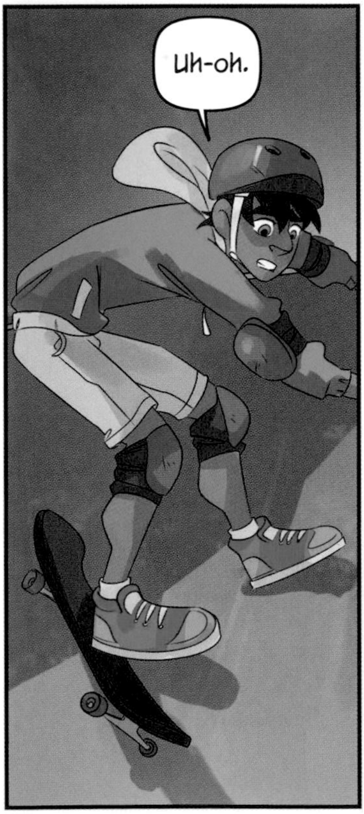
Uh-oh.

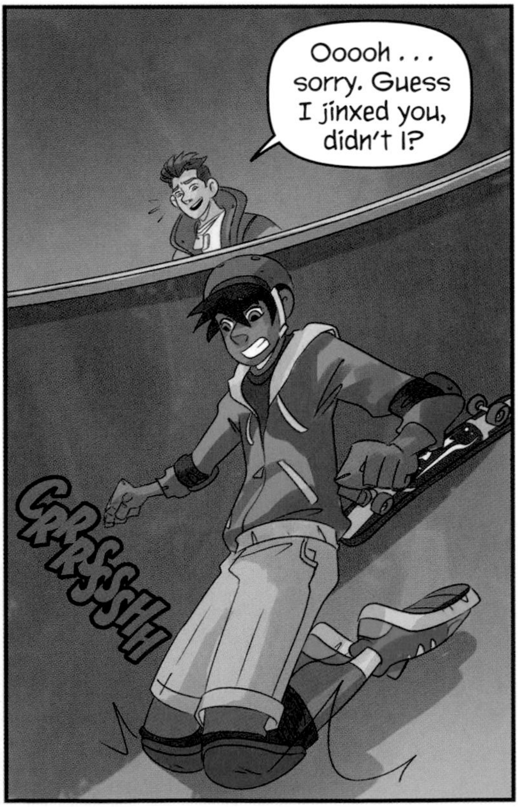
Ooooh . . . sorry. Guess I jinxed you, didn't I?
CRRSSSHH

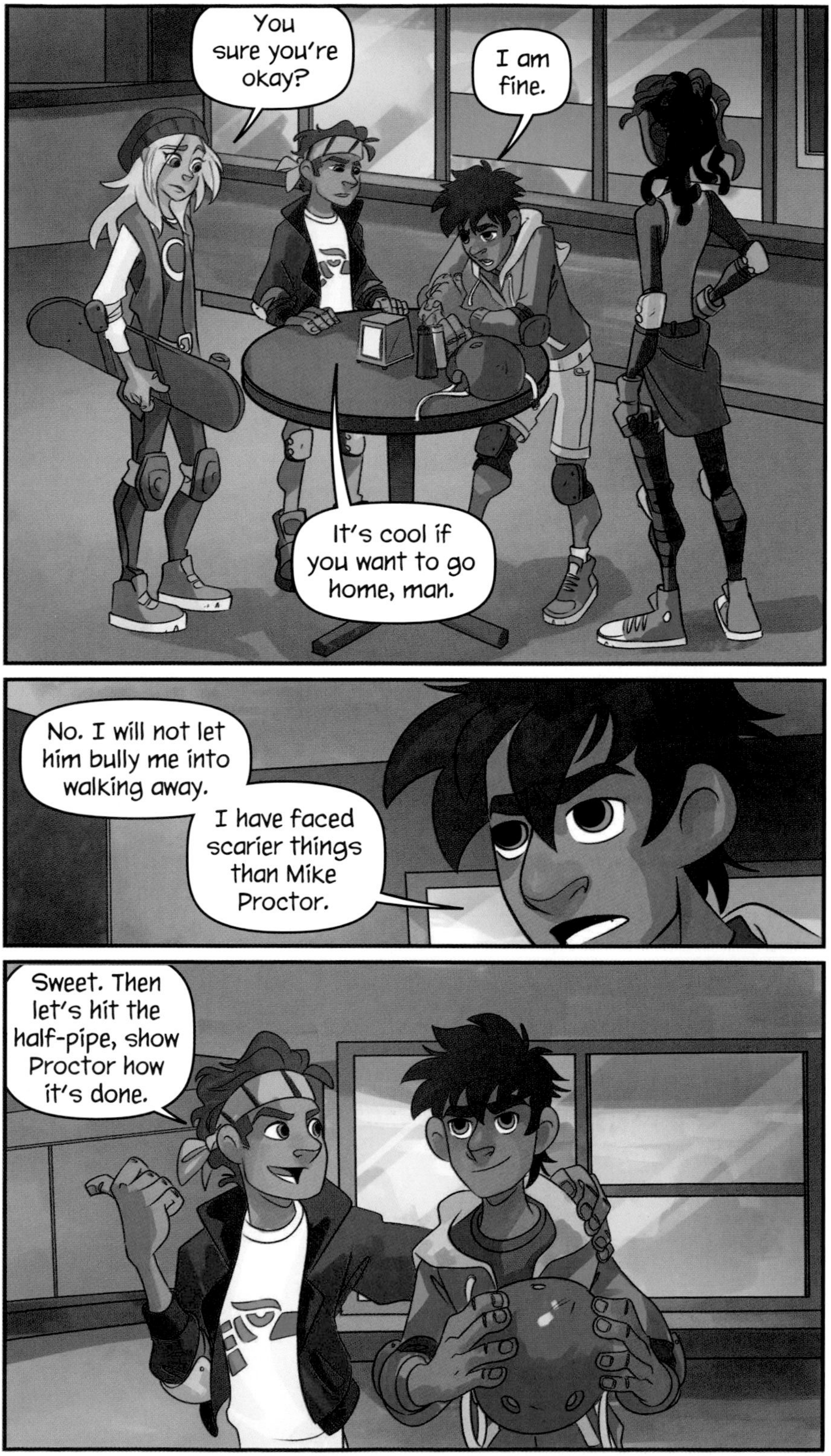
You sure you're okay?
I am fine.
It's cool if you want to go home, man.
No. I will not let him bully me into walking away.
I have faced scarier things than Mike Proctor.
Sweet. Then let's hit the half-pipe, show Proctor how it's done.

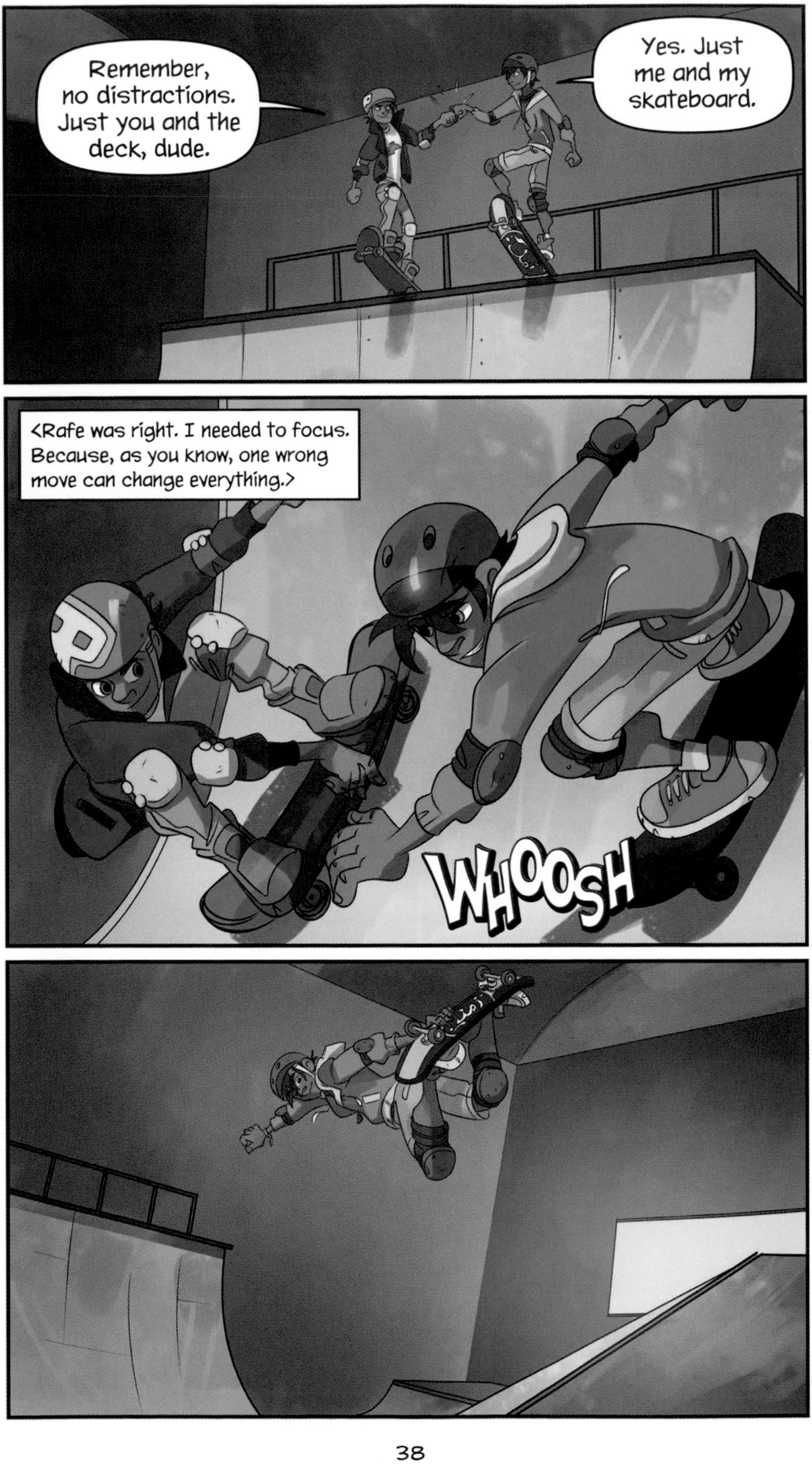
Remember, no distractions. Just you and the deck, dude.
Yes. Just me and my skateboard.
<Rafe was right. I needed to focus. Because, as you know, one wrong move can change everything.>
WHOOSH

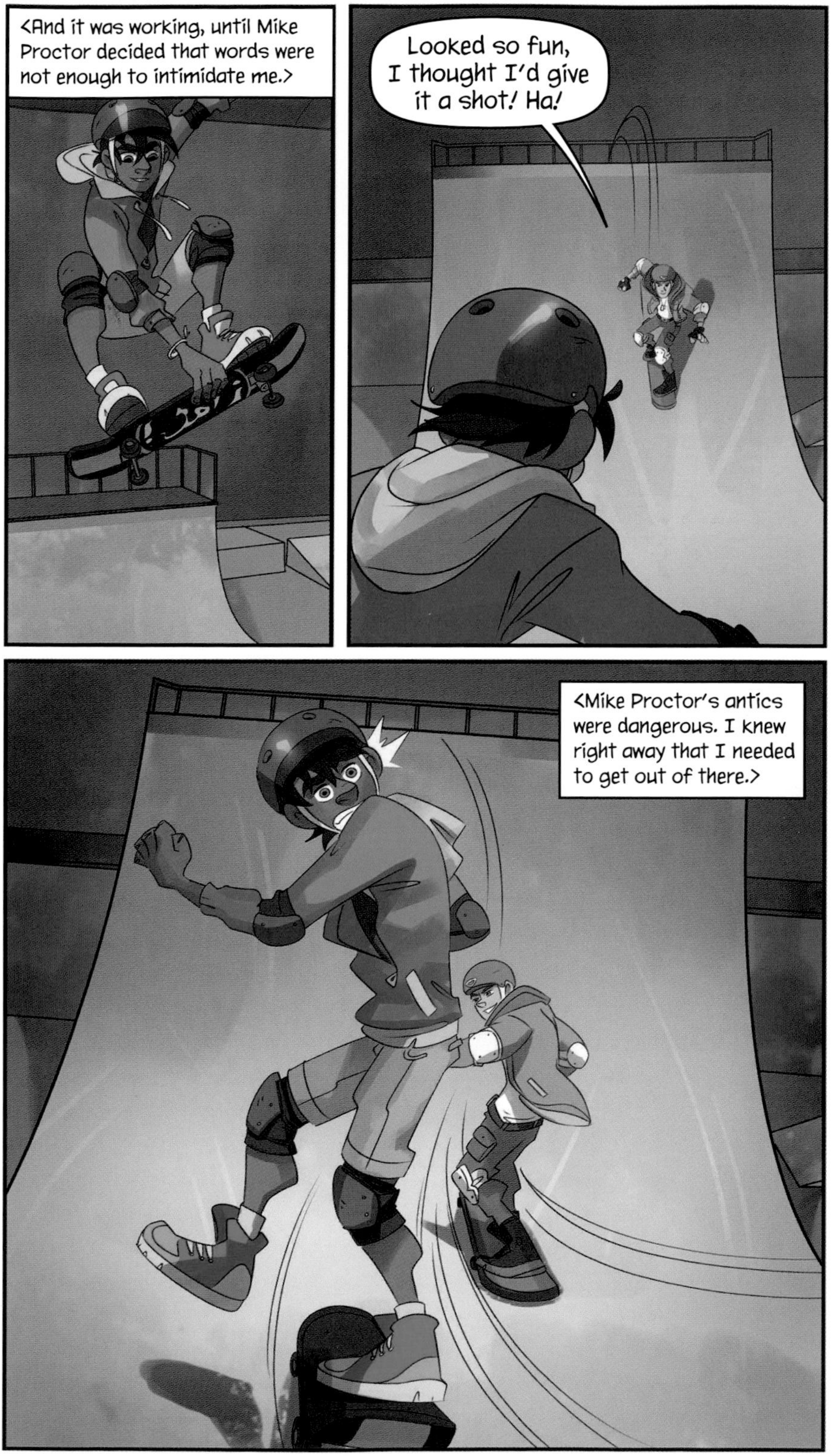
<And it was working, until Mike Proctor decided that words were not enough to intimidate me.>
Looked so fun, I thought I'd give it a shot! Ha!
<Mike Proctor's antics were dangerous. I knew right away that I needed to get out of there.>

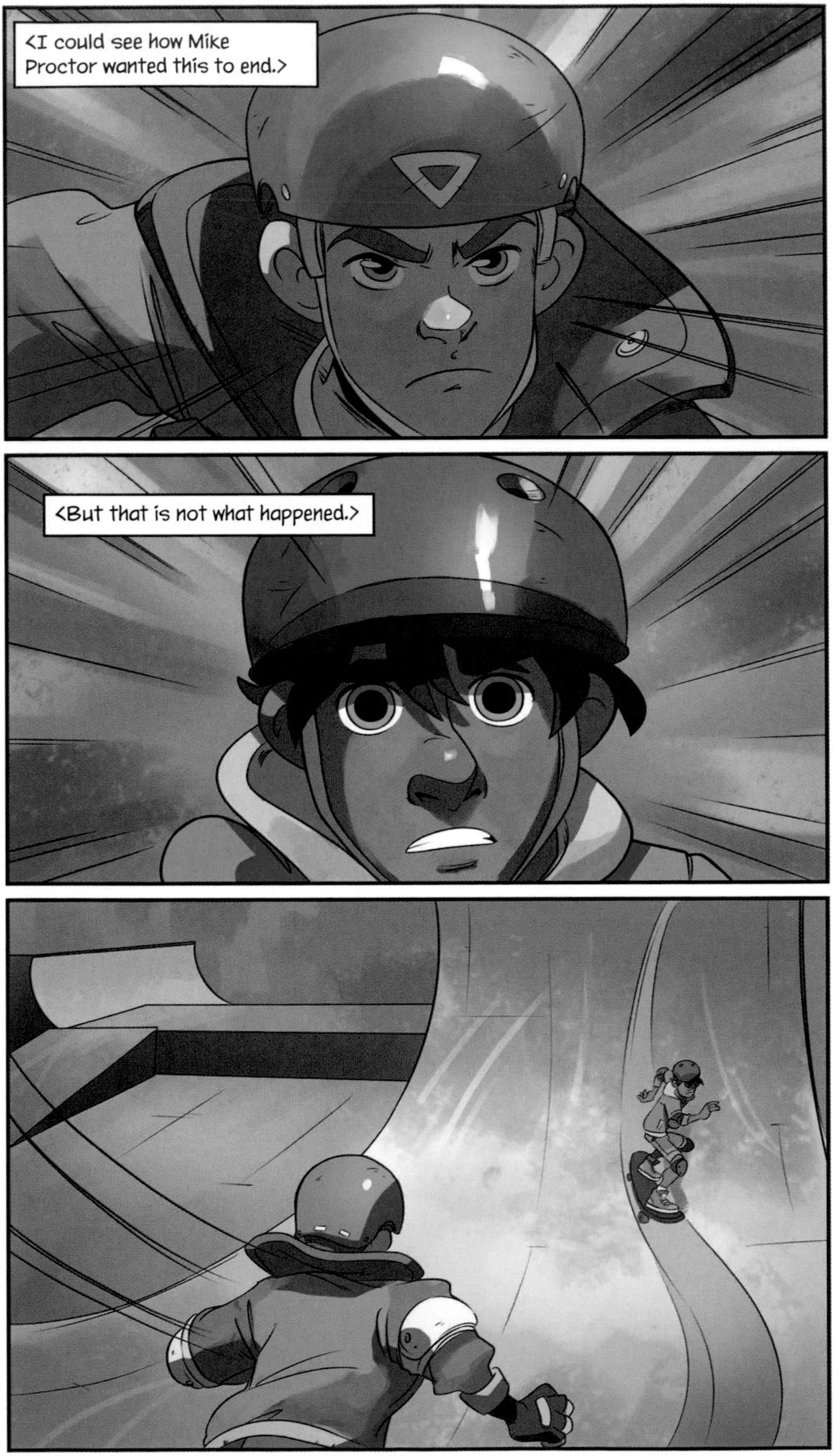
<I could see how Mike Proctor wanted this to end.>
<But that is not what happened.>

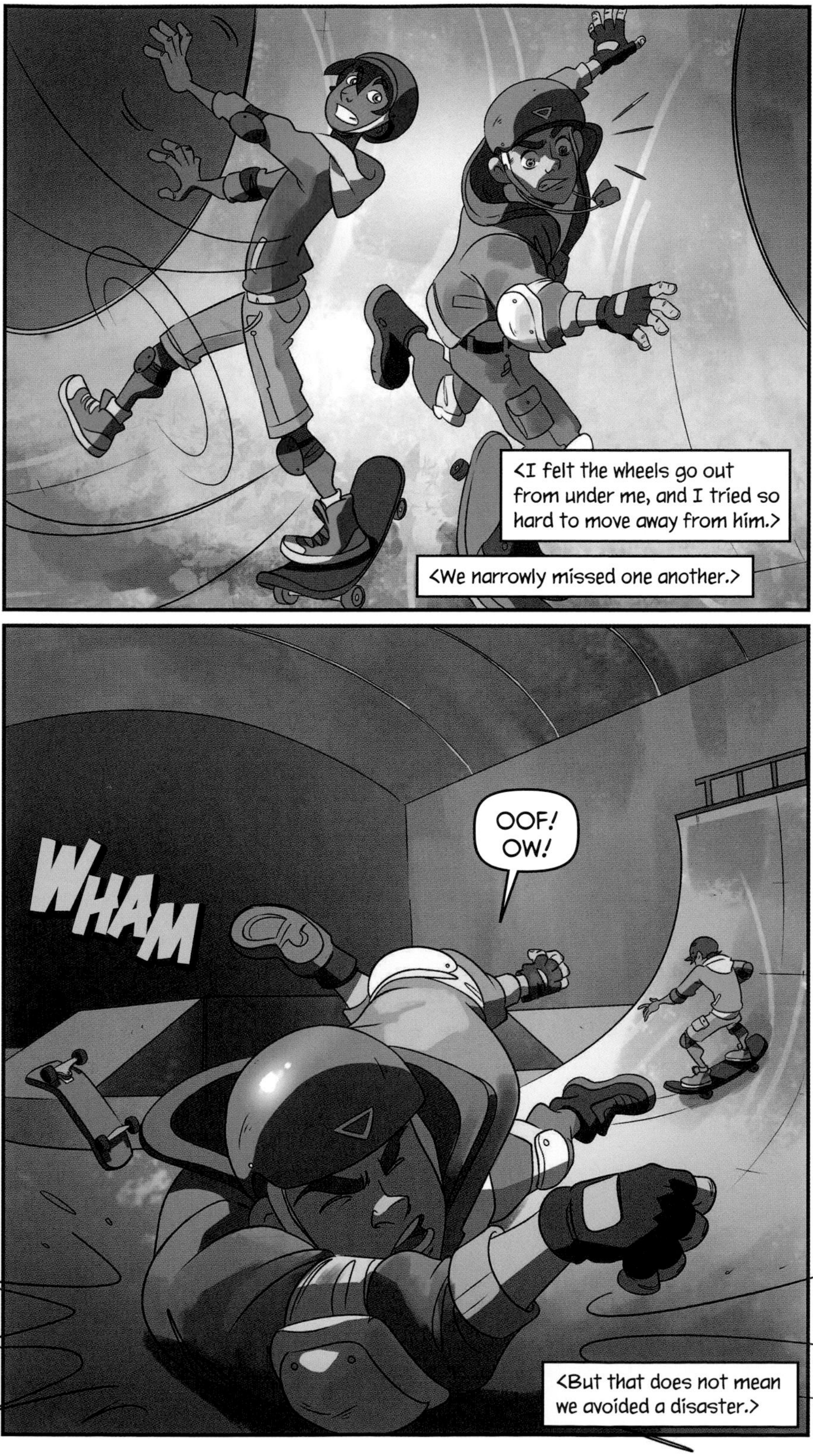
<I felt the wheels go out from under me, and I tried so hard to move away from him.>
<We narrowly missed one another.>
WHAM
OOF! OW!
<But that does not mean we avoided a disaster.>

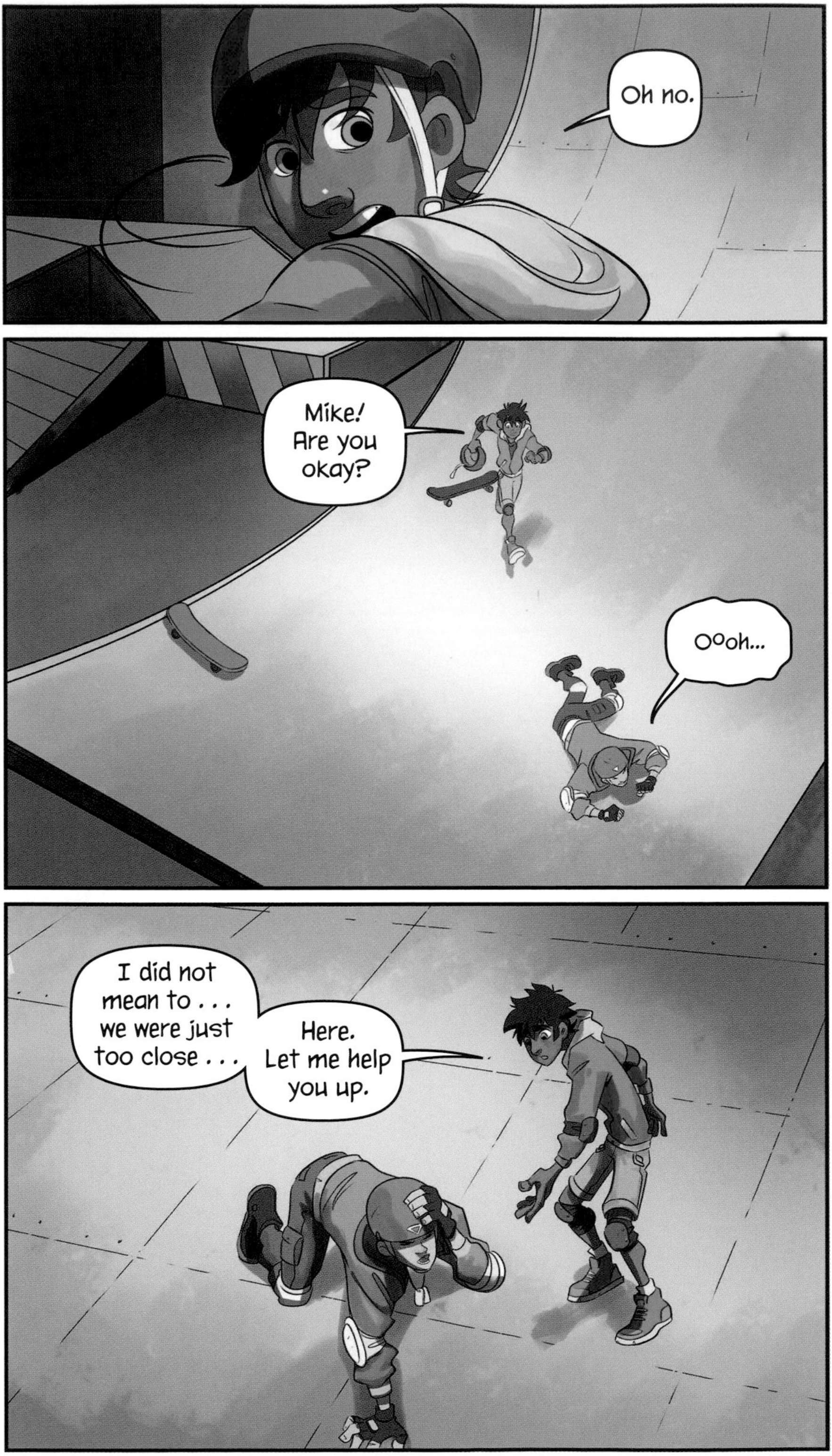
Oh no.
Mike! Are you okay?
Oooh...
I did not mean to . . . we were just too close . . .
Here. Let me help you up.

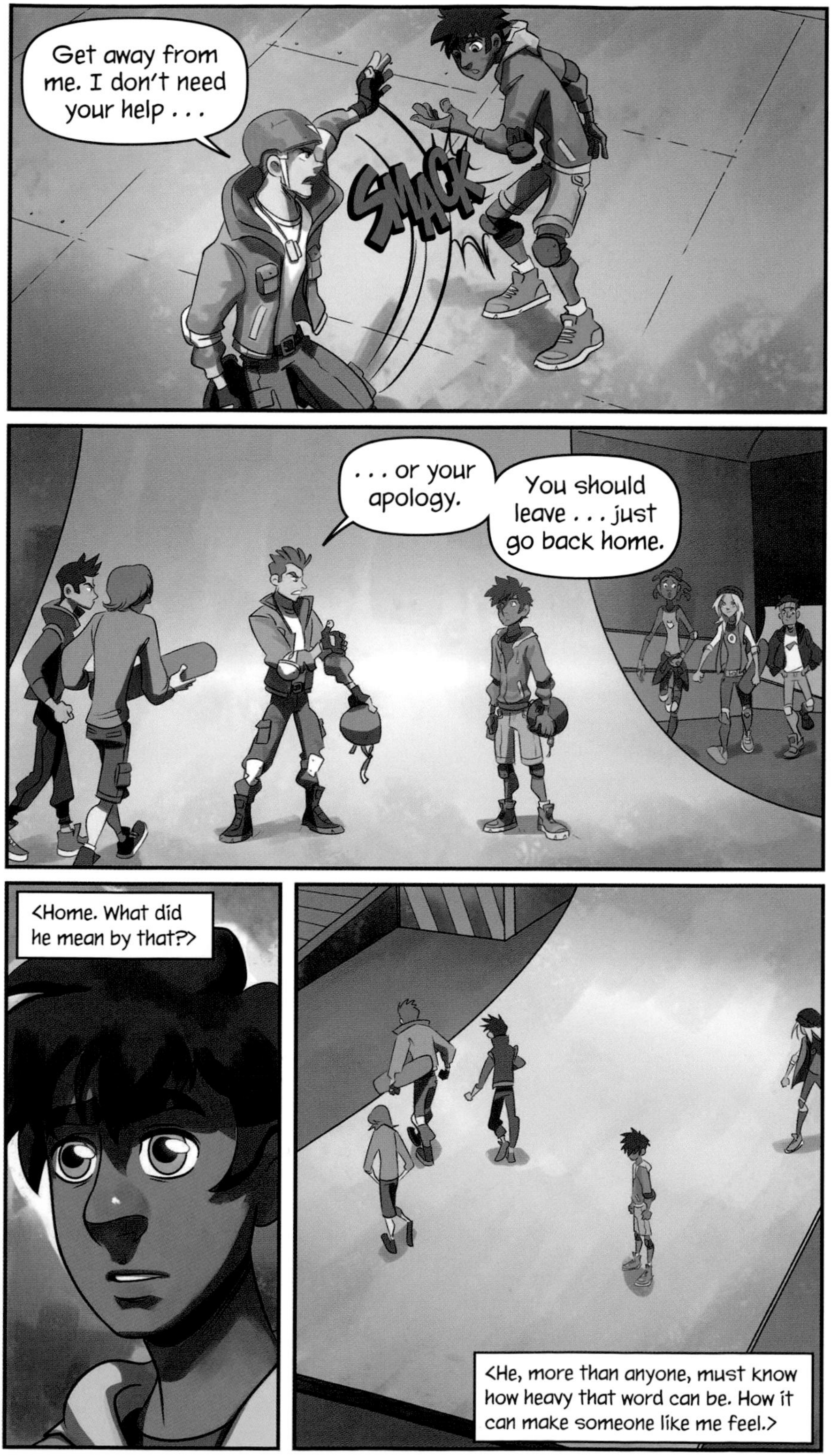

Get away from me. I don't need your help . . .
SMACK
. . . or your apology.
You should leave . . . just go back home.
<Home. What did he mean by that?>
<He, more than anyone, must know how heavy that word can be. How it can make someone like me feel.>

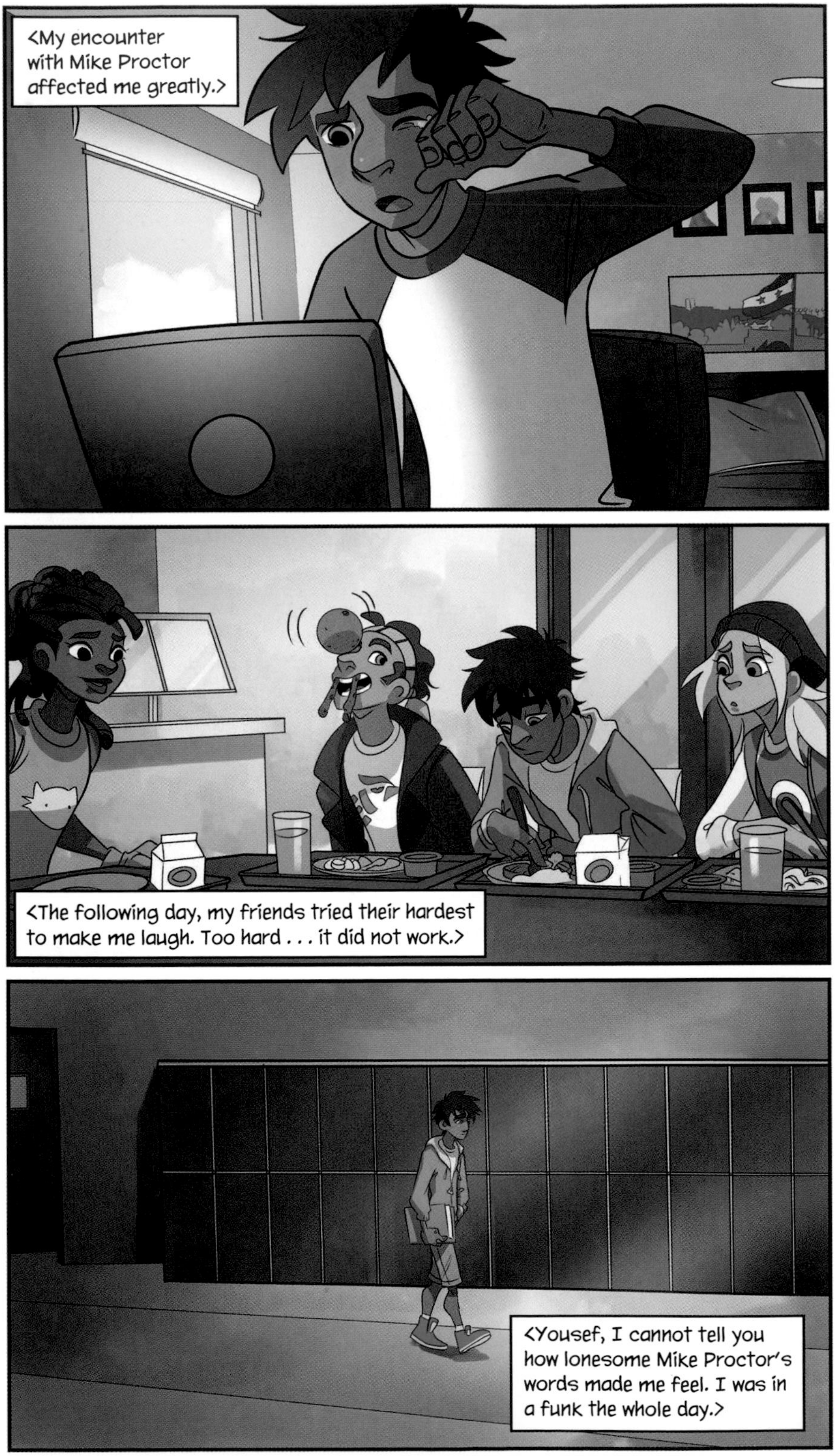
<My encounter with Mike Proctor affected me greatly.>
<The following day, my friends tried their hardest to make me laugh. Too hard . . . it did not work.>
<Yousef, I cannot tell you how lonesome Mike Proctor's words made me feel. I was in a funk the whole day.>

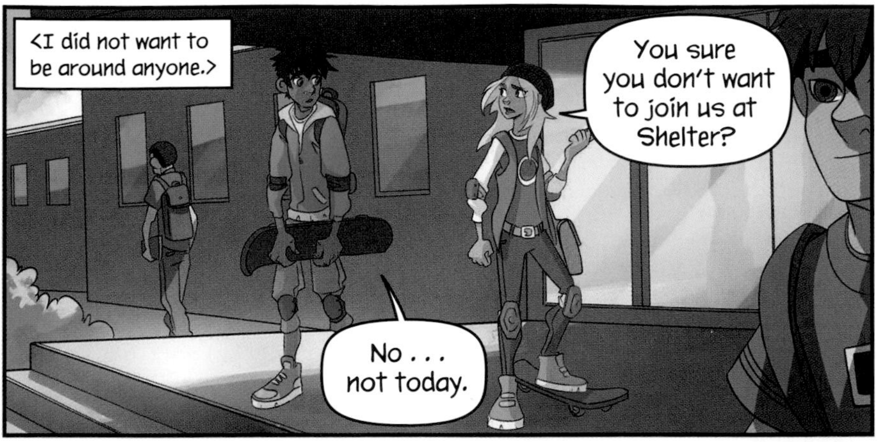
<I did not want to be around anyone.>
You sure you don't want to join us at Shelter?
No . . . not today.

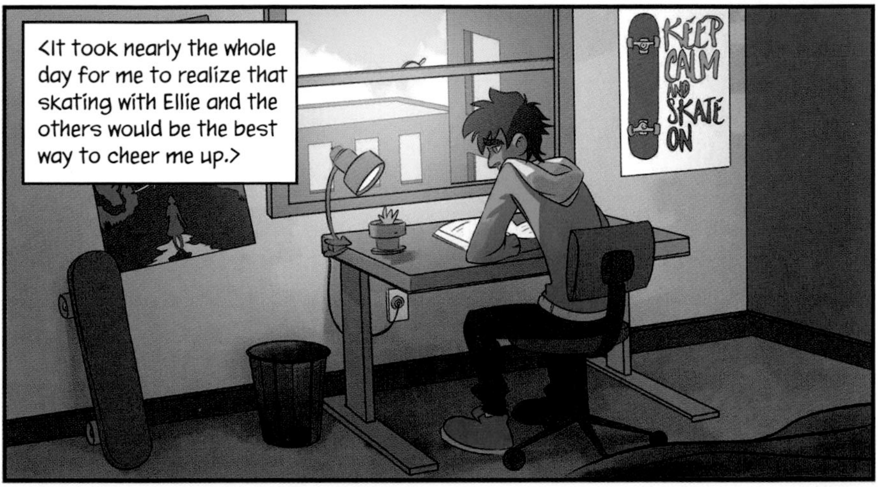
<It took nearly the whole day for me to realize that skating with Ellie and the others would be the best way to cheer me up.>
KEEP CALM AND SKATE ON

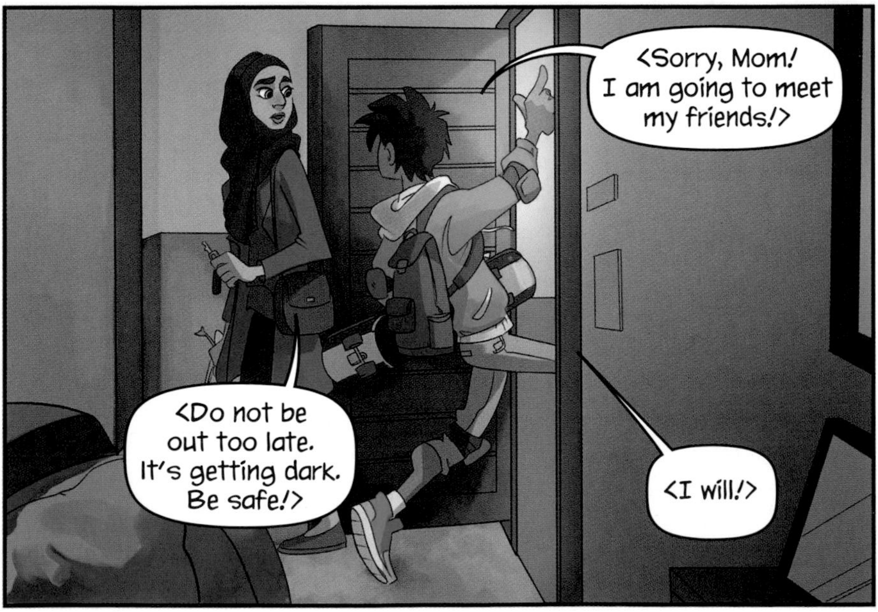
<Sorry, Mom! I am going to meet my friends!>
<Do not be out too late. It's getting dark. Be safe!>
<I will!>

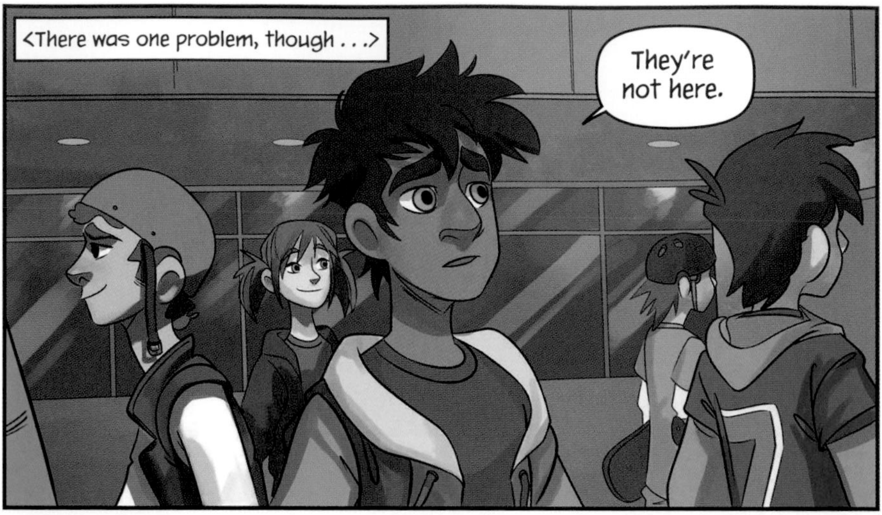
<There was one problem, though . . .>
They're not here.

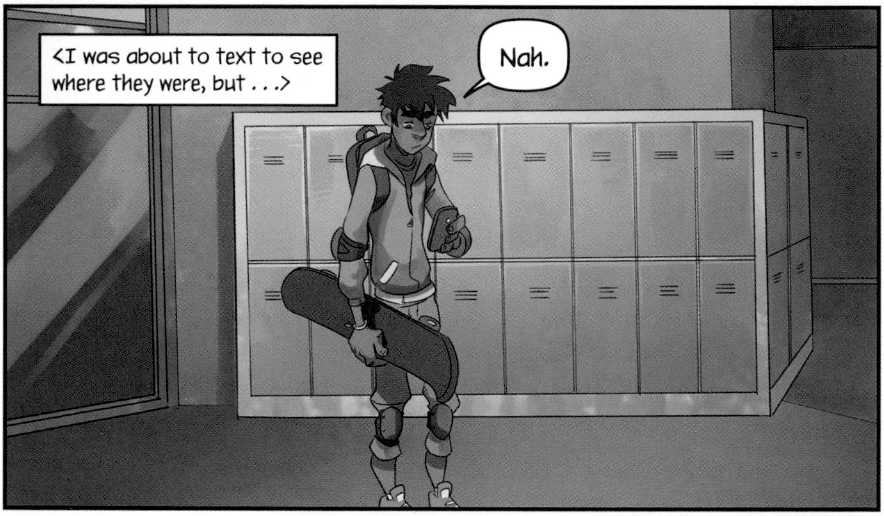
<I was about to text to see where they were, but . . .>
Nah.

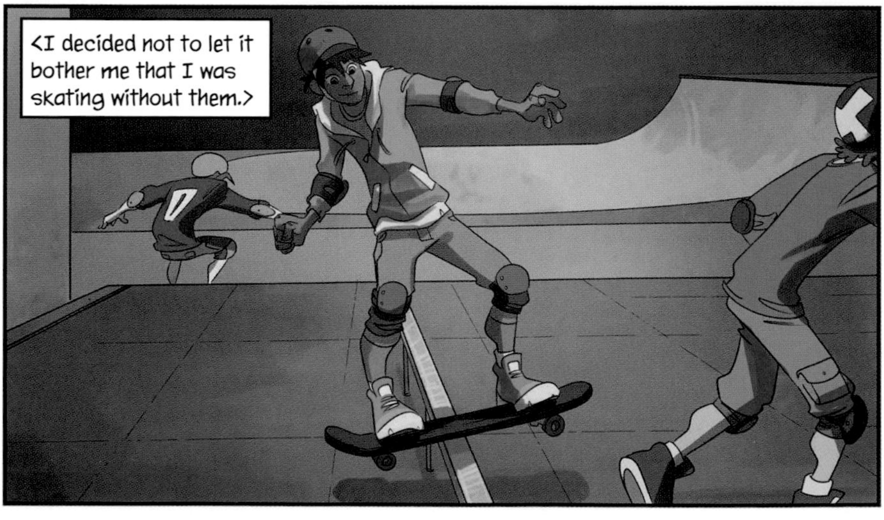
<I decided not to let it bother me that I was skating without them.>

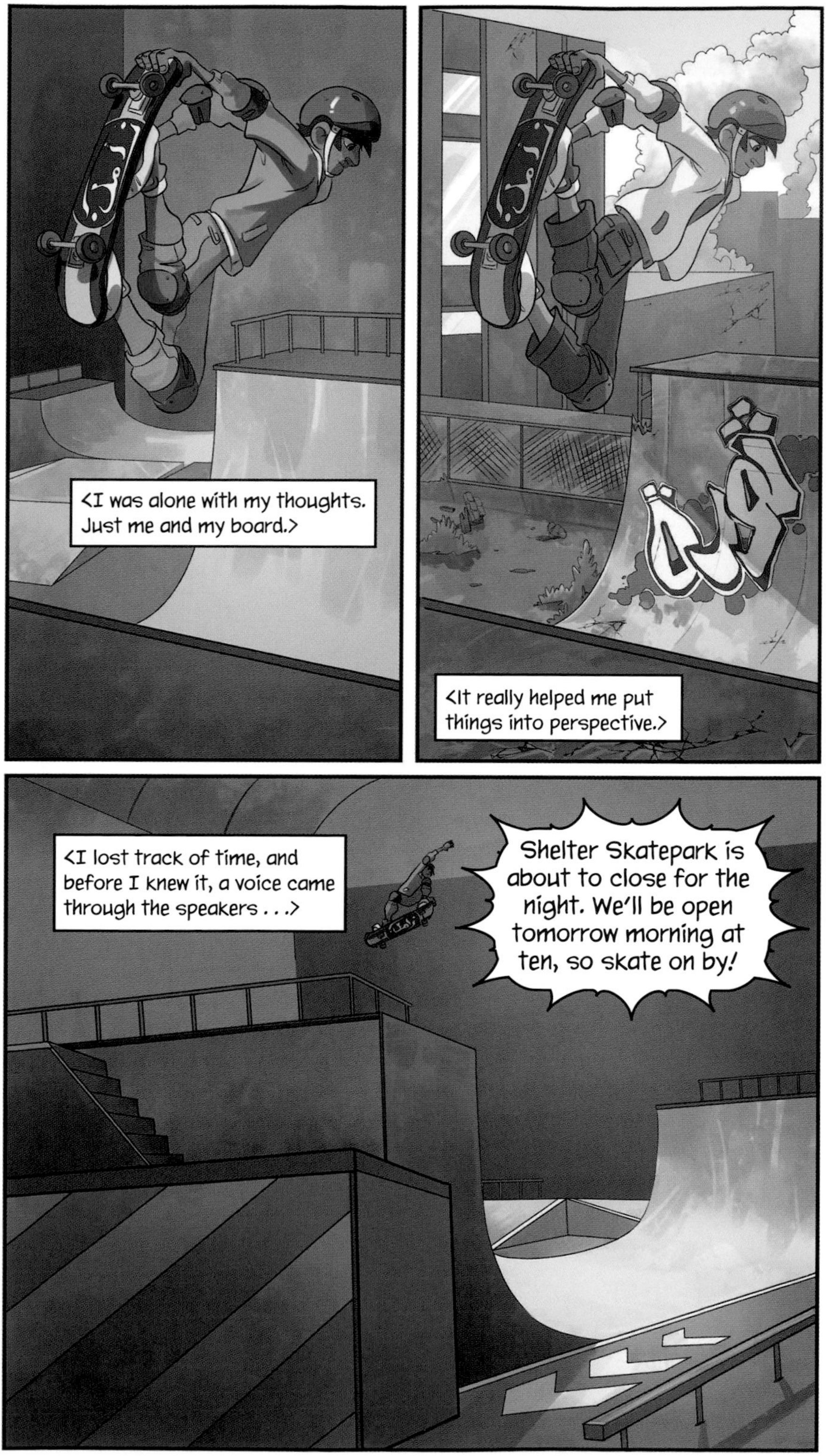
<I was alone with my thoughts. Just me and my board.>
<It really helped me put things into perspective.>
<I lost track of time, and before I knew it, a voice came through the speakers . . .>
Shelter Skatepark is about to close for the night. We'll be open tomorrow morning at ten, so skate on by!

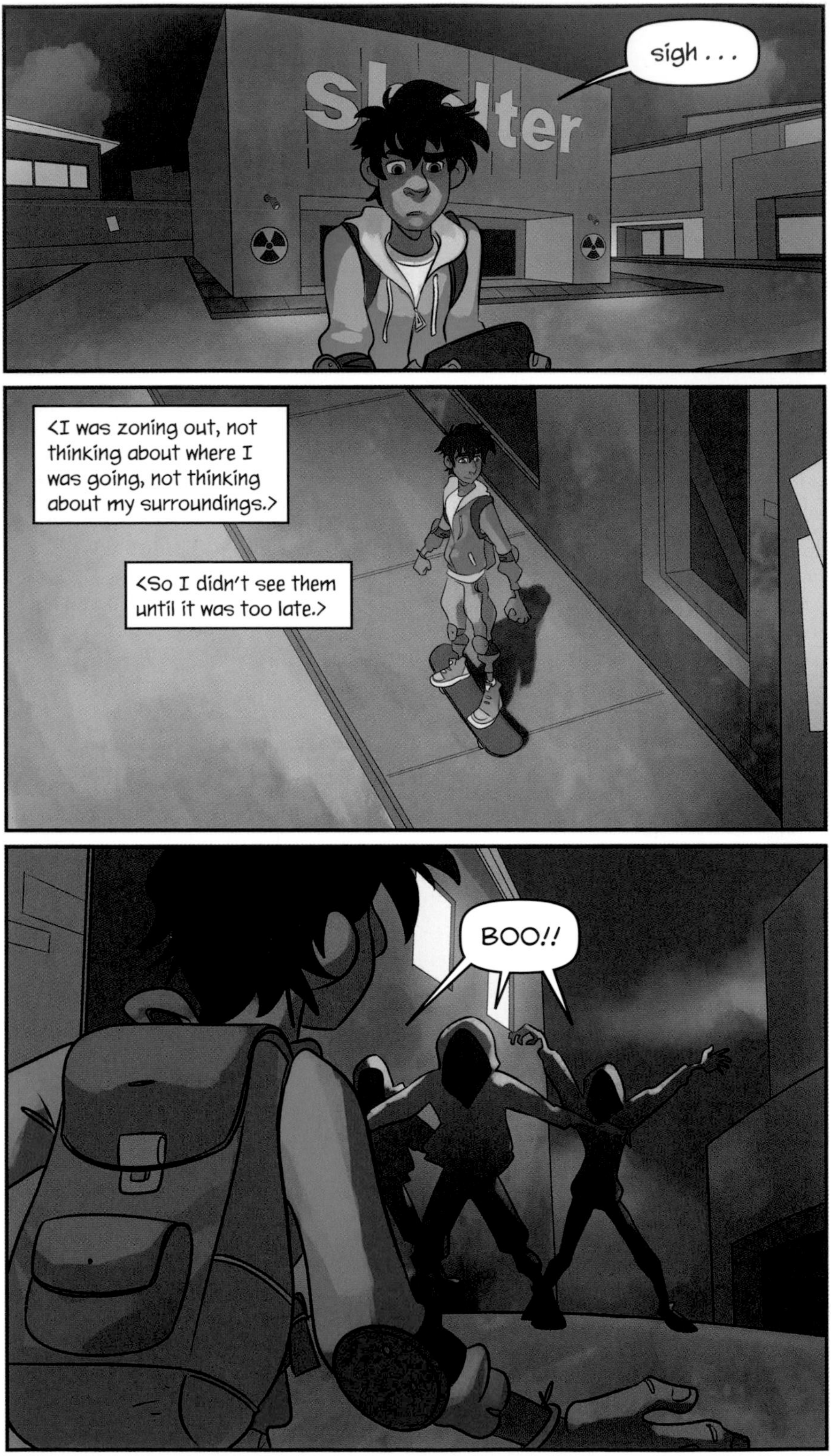

sigh . . .
<I was zoning out, not thinking about where I was going, not thinking about my surroundings.>
<So I didn't see them until it was too late.>
BOO!!

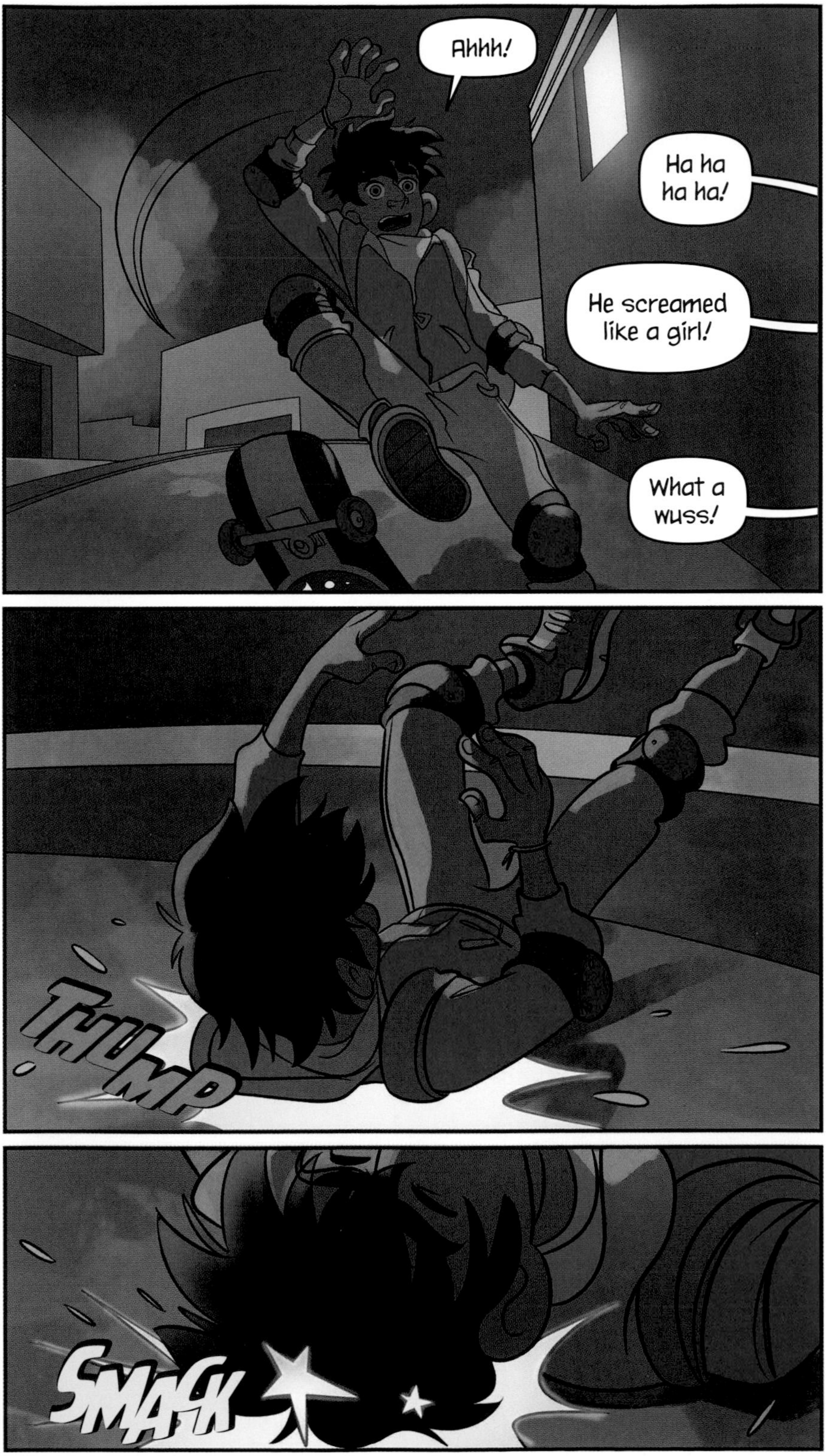
Ahhh!
Ha ha ha ha!
He screamed like a girl!
What a wuss!
THUMP
SMACK

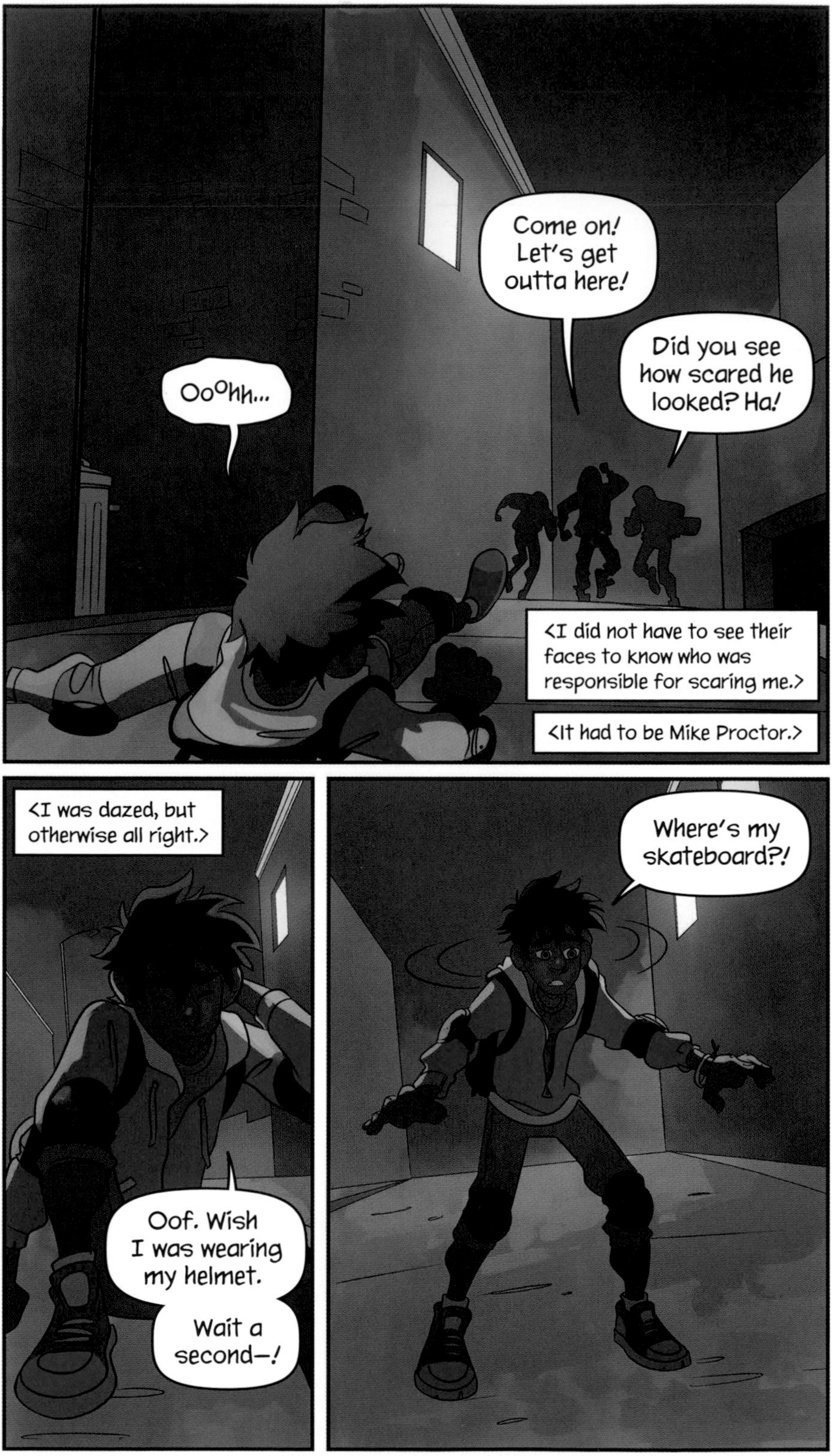
Oooohh...
Come on! Let's get outta here!
Did you see how scared he looked? Ha!
<I did not have to see their faces to know who was responsible for scaring me.>
<It had to be Mike Proctor.>
<I was dazed, but otherwise all right.>
Oof. Wish I was wearing my helmet.
Wait a second—!
Where's my skateboard?!

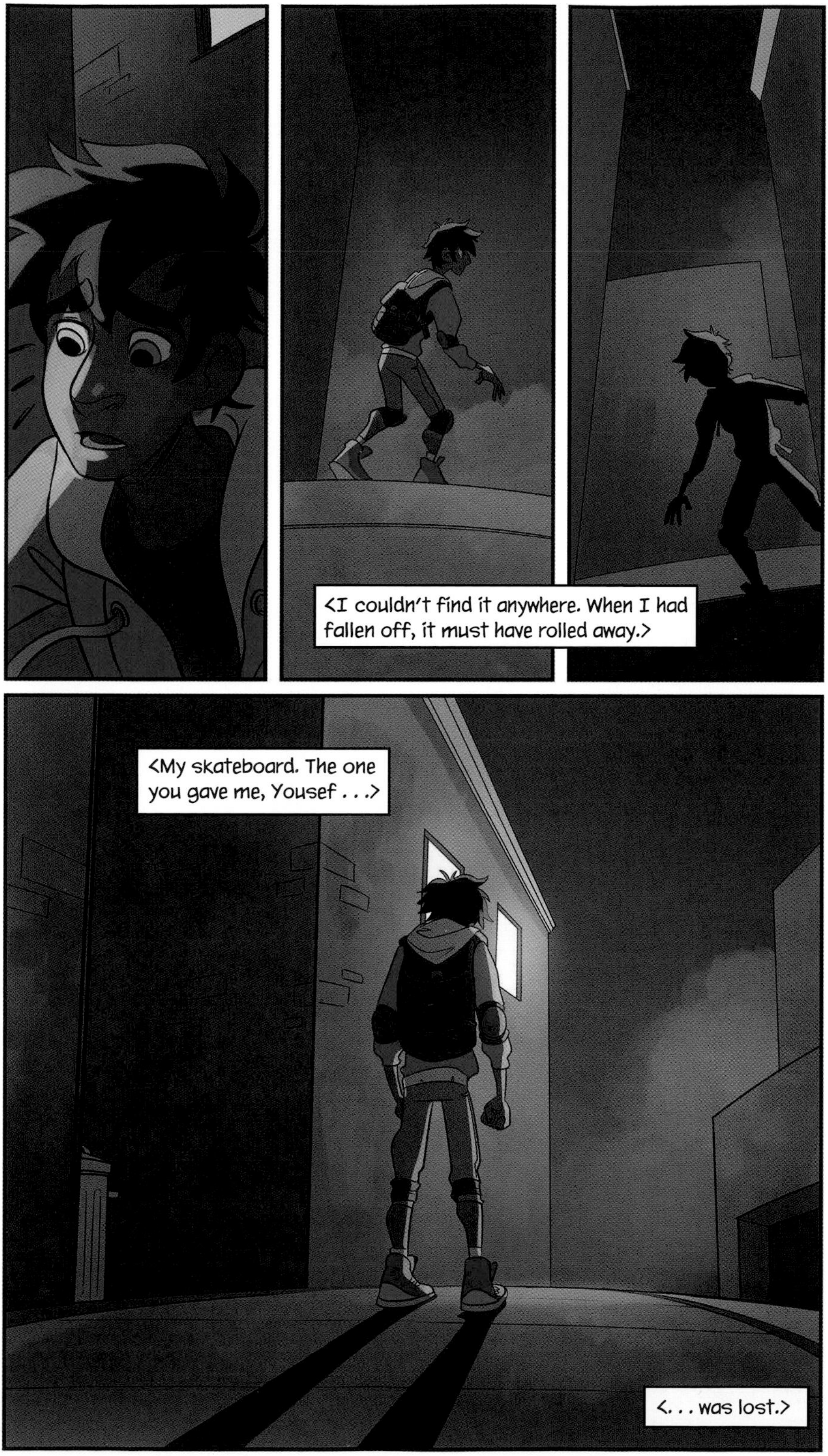
<I couldn't find it anywhere. When I had fallen off, it must have rolled away.>
<My skateboard. The one you gave me, Yousef . . .>
<. . . was lost.>

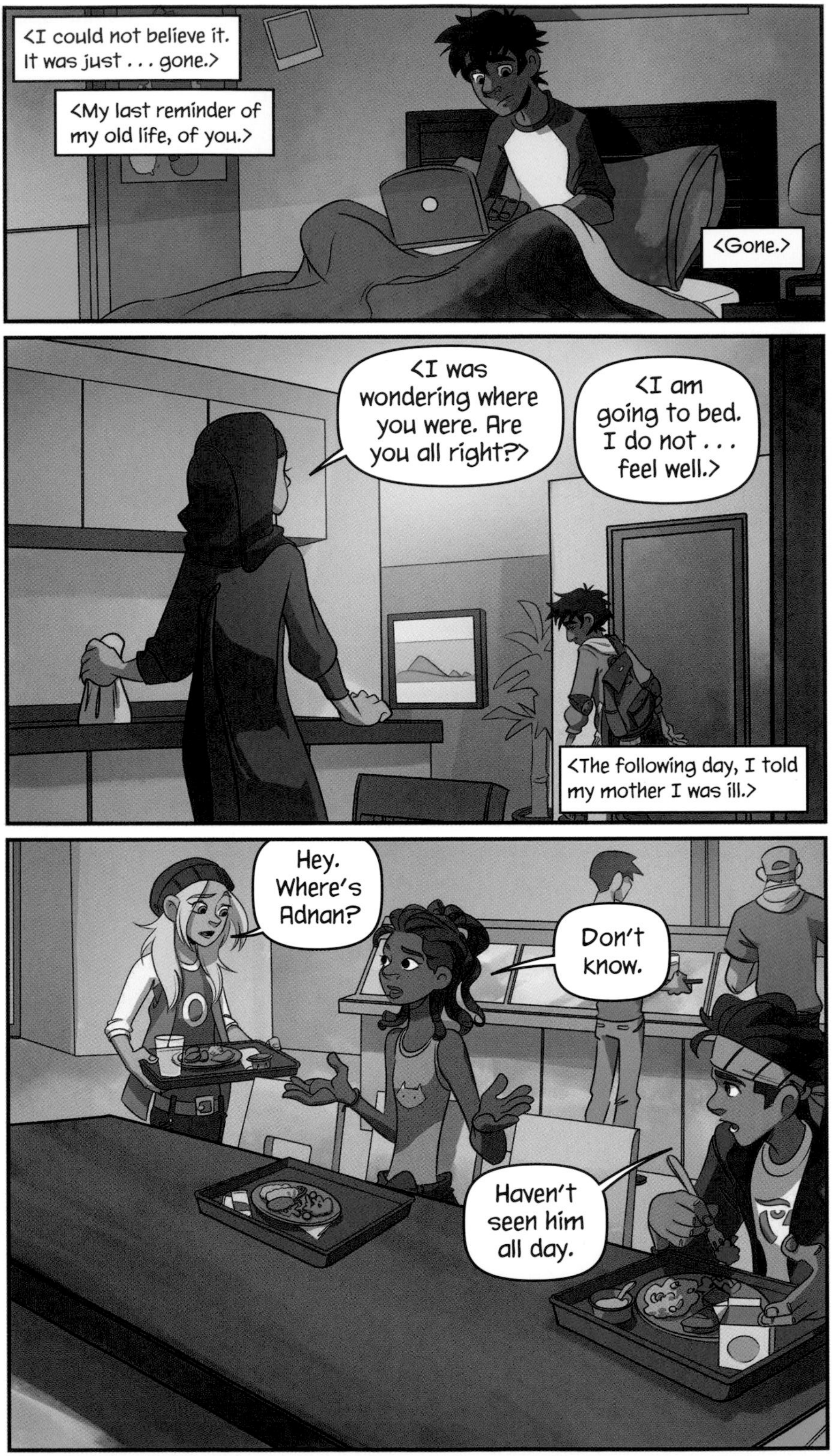
<I could not believe it. It was just . . . gone.>
<My last reminder of my old life, of you.>
<Gone.>
<I was wondering where you were. Are you all right?>
<I am going to bed. I do not . . . feel well.>
<The following day, I told my mother I was ill.>
Hey. Where's Adnan?
Don't know.
Haven't seen him all day.

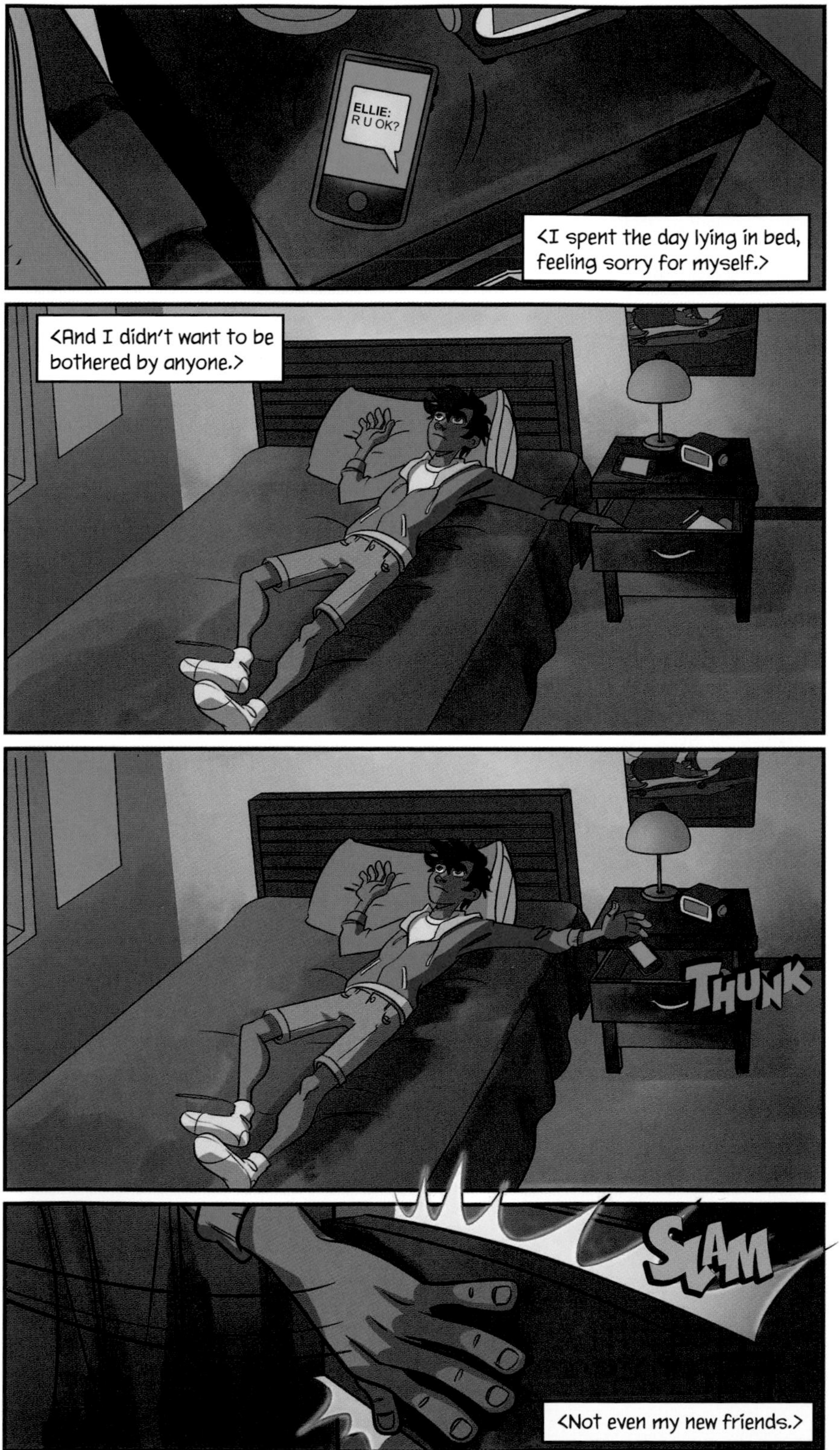
ELLIE:
R U OK?
<I spent the day lying in bed, feeling sorry for myself.>
<And I didn't want to be bothered by anyone.>
THUNK
SLAM
<Not even my new friends.>

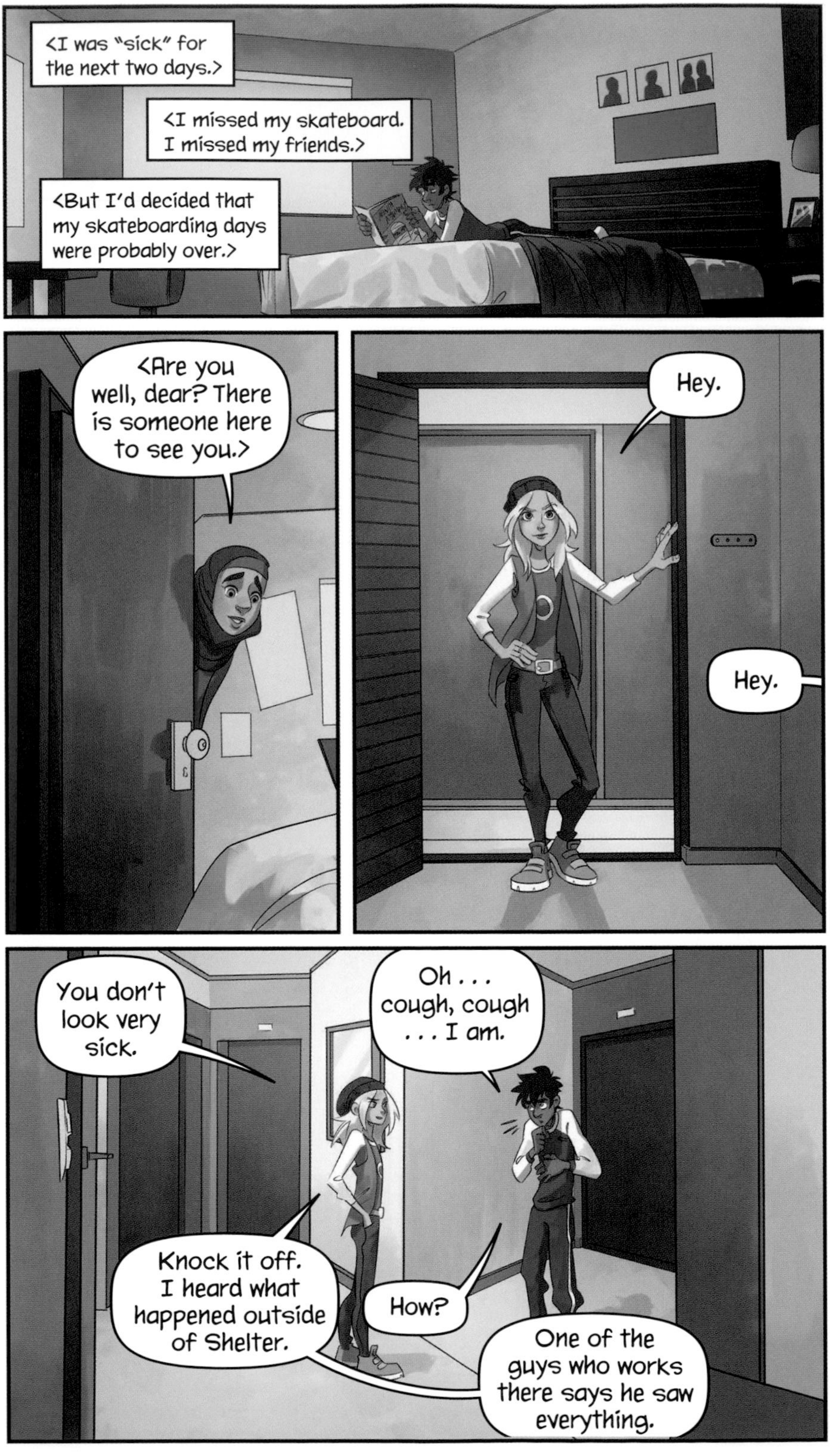
<I was "sick" for the next two days.>
<I missed my skateboard. I missed my friends.>
<But I'd decided that my skateboarding days were probably over.>
<Are you well, dear? There is someone here to see you.>
Hey.
Hey.
You don't look very sick.
Oh . . . cough, cough . . . I am.
Knock it off. I heard what happened outside of Shelter.
How?
One of the guys who works there says he saw everything.

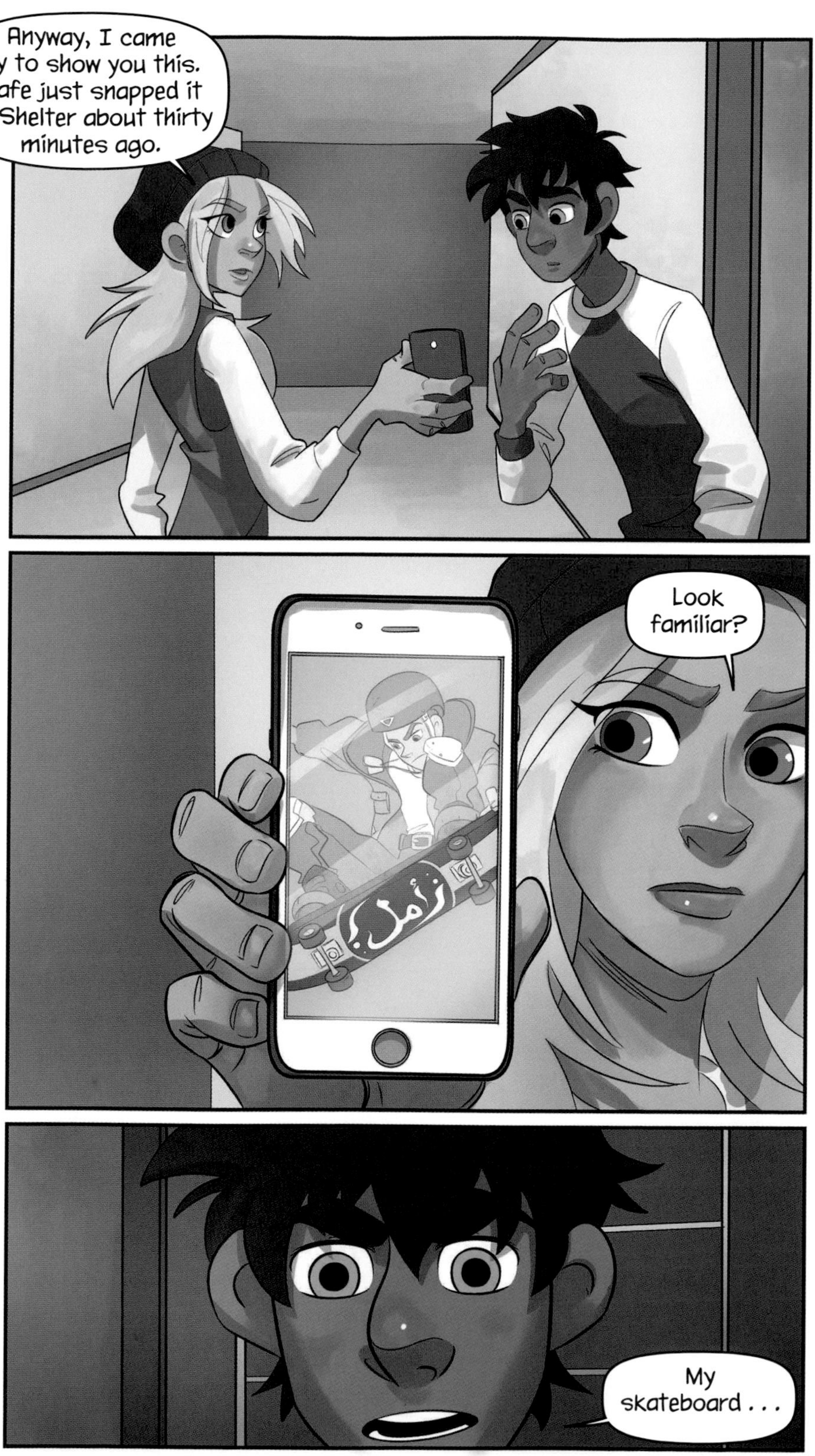
Anyway, I came by to show you this. Rafe just snapped it at Shelter about thirty minutes ago.
Look familiar?
My skateboard . . .

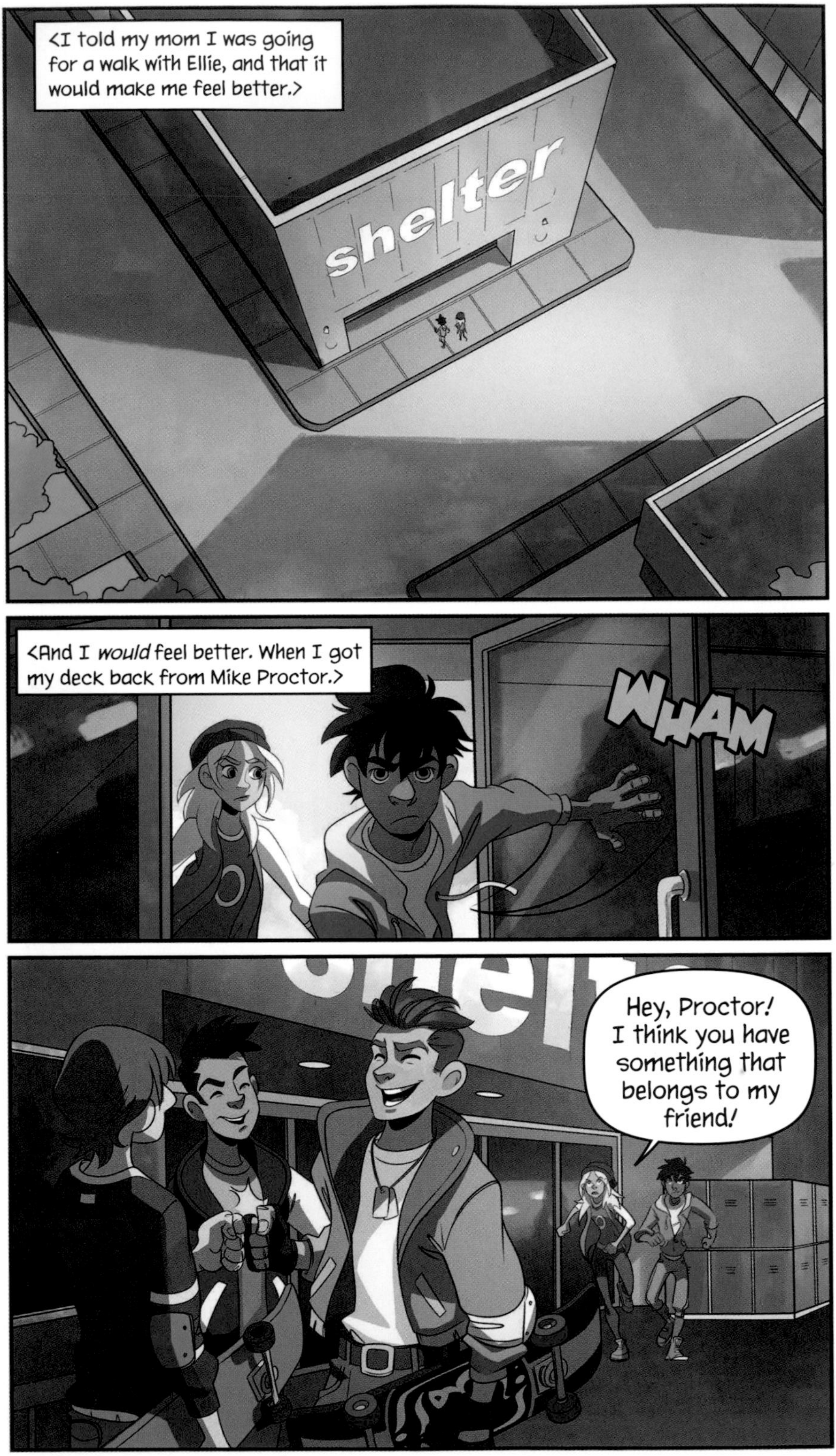

<I told my mom I was going for a walk with Ellie, and that it would make me feel better.>
shelter
<And I *would* feel better. When I got my deck back from Mike Proctor.>
WHAM
Hey, Proctor! I think you have something that belongs to my friend!

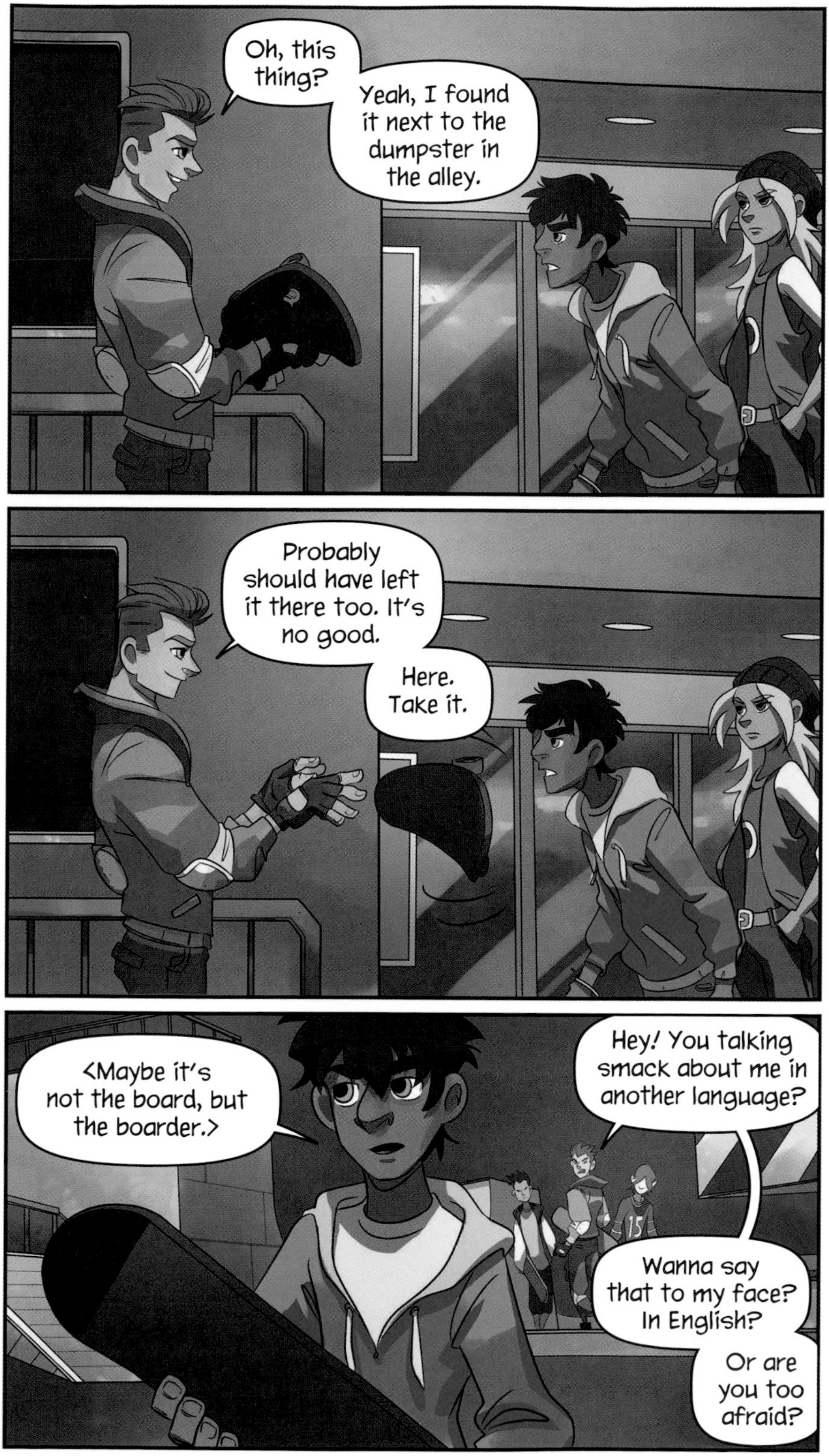

Oh, this thing?
Yeah, I found it next to the dumpster in the alley.
Probably should have left it there too. It's no good.
Here. Take it.
<Maybe it's not the board, but the boarder.>
Hey! You talking smack about me in another language?
Wanna say that to my face? In English?
Or are you too afraid?

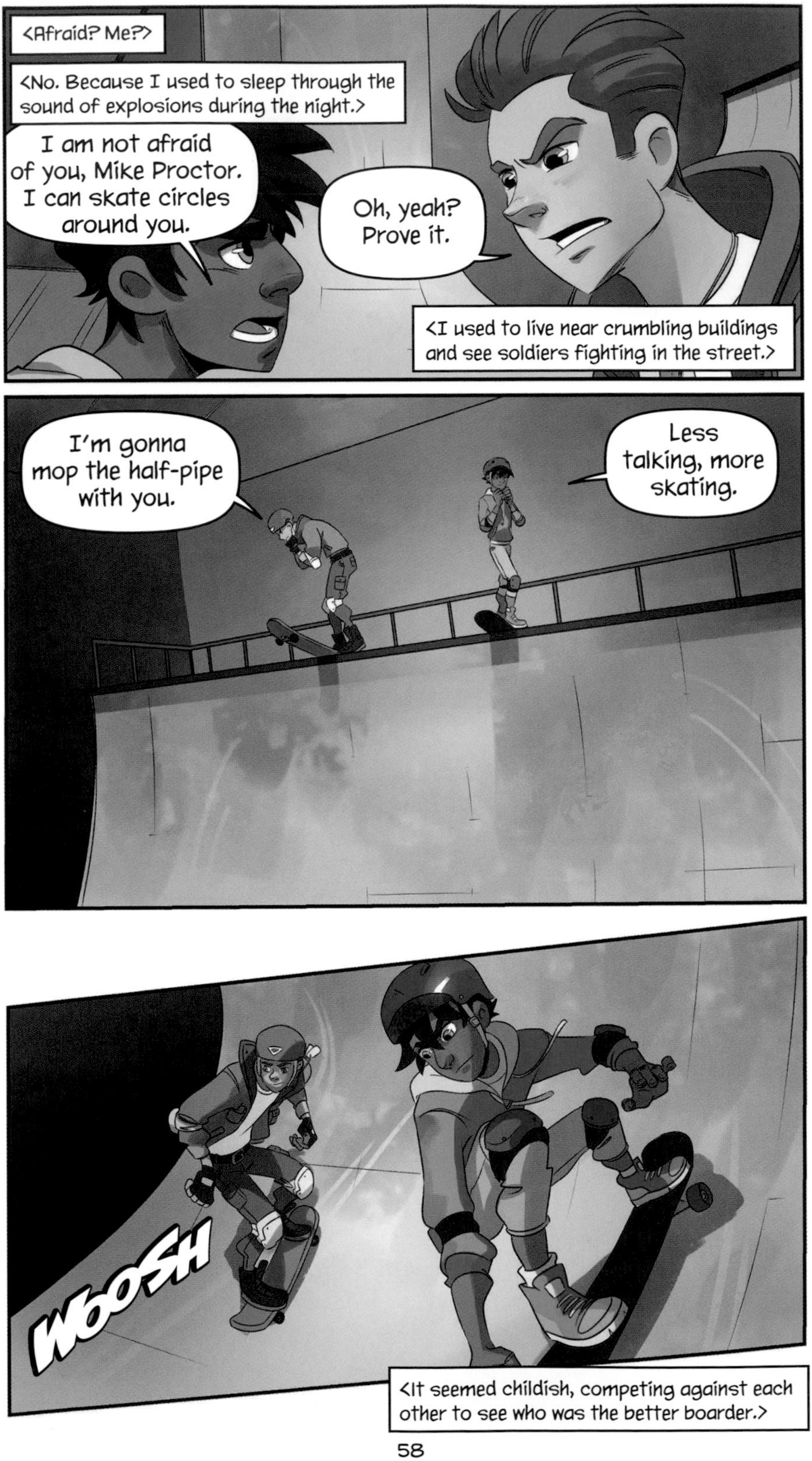
<Afraid? Me?>
<No. Because I used to sleep through the sound of explosions during the night.>
I am not afraid of you, Mike Proctor. I can skate circles around you.
Oh, yeah? Prove it.
<I used to live near crumbling buildings and see soldiers fighting in the street.>
I'm gonna mop the half-pipe with you.
Less talking, more skating.
WOOSH
<It seemed childish, competing against each other to see who was the better boarder.>

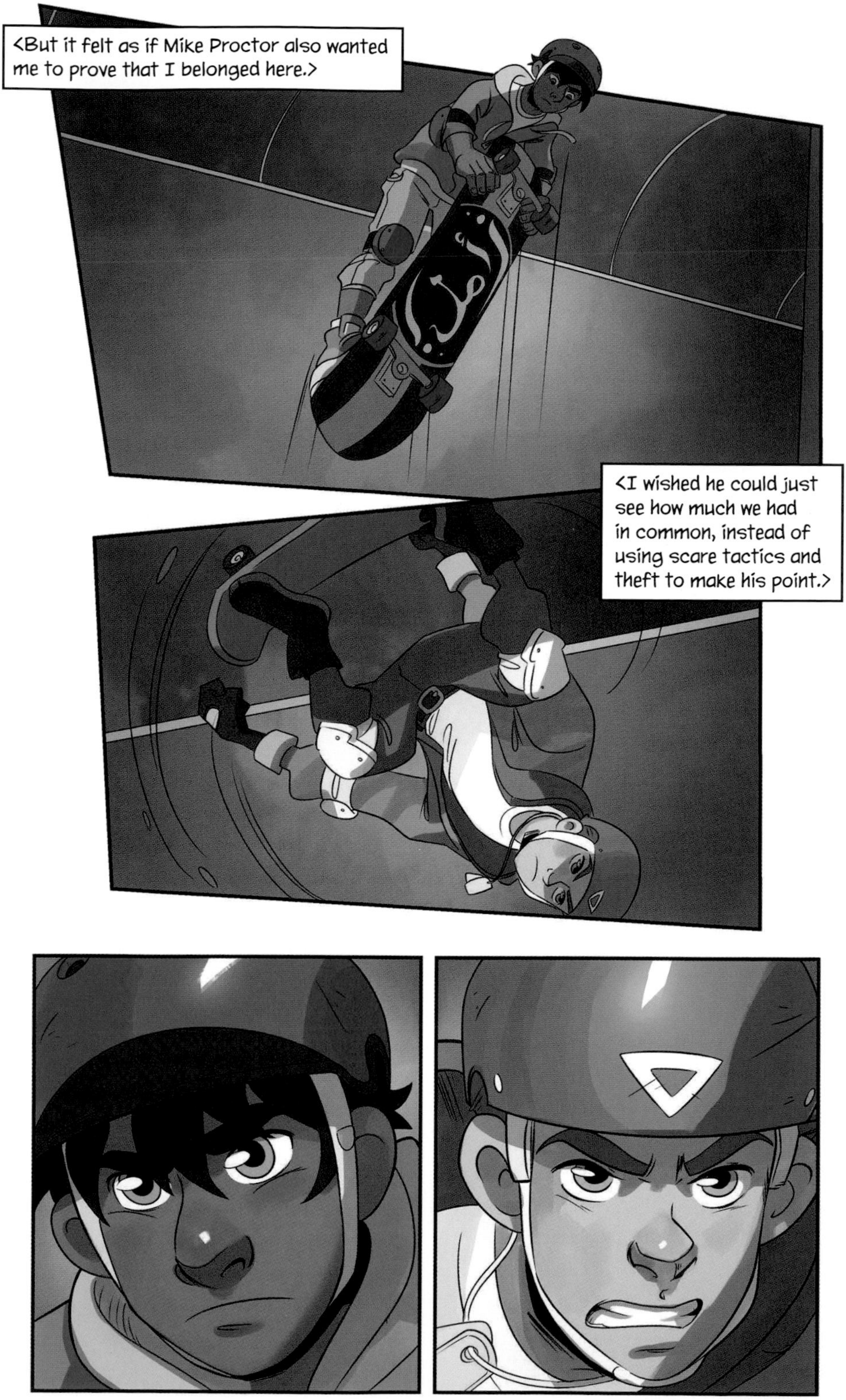
<But it felt as if Mike Proctor also wanted me to prove that I belonged here.>
<I wished he could just see how much we had in common, instead of using scare tactics and theft to make his point.>

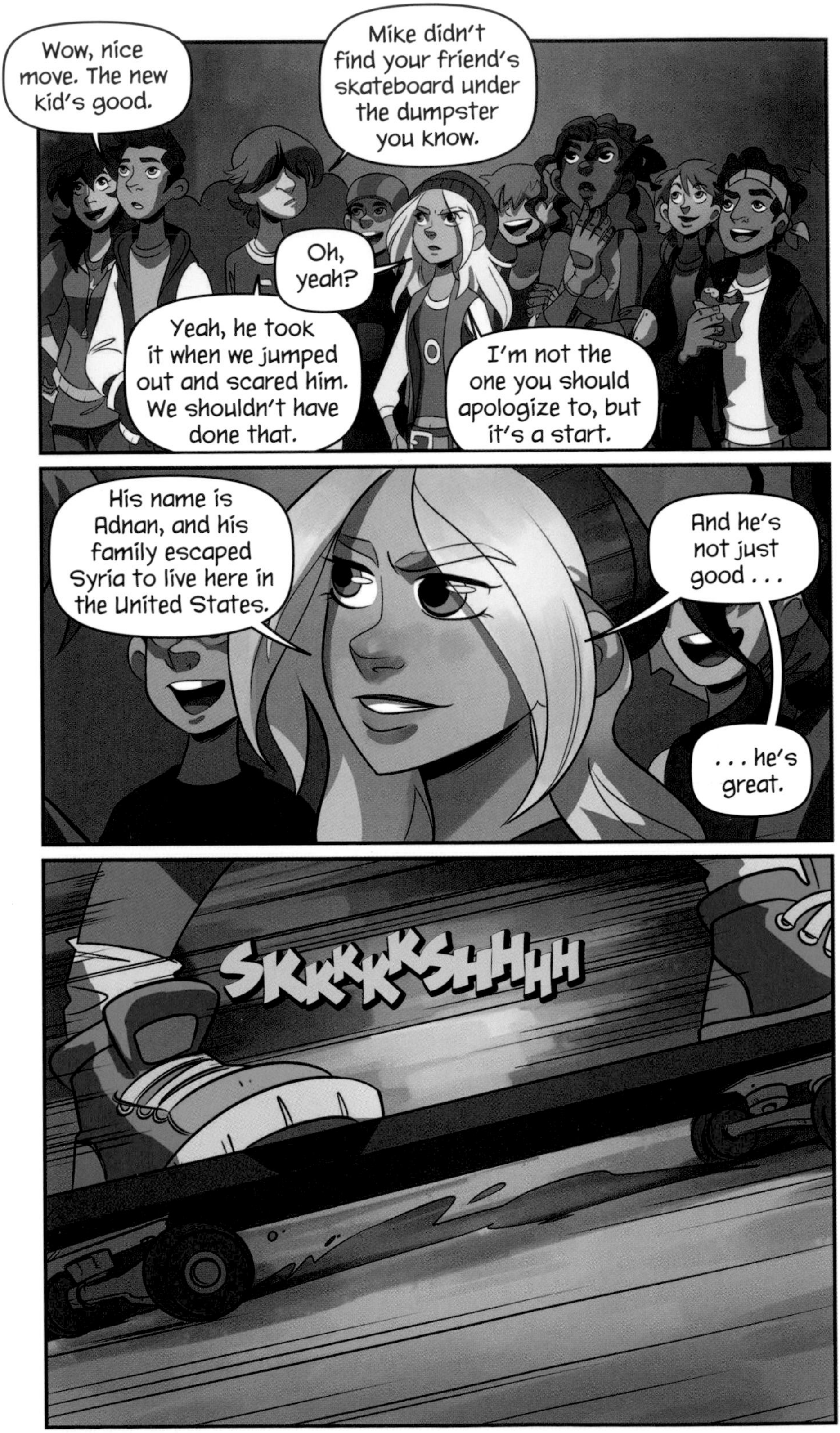
Wow, nice move. The new kid's good.
Mike didn't find your friend's skateboard under the dumpster you know.
Oh, yeah?
Yeah, he took it when we jumped out and scared him. We shouldn't have done that.
I'm not the one you should apologize to, but it's a start.
His name is Adnan, and his family escaped Syria to live here in the United States.
And he's not just good . . .
. . . he's great.
SKKKKKSHHHH

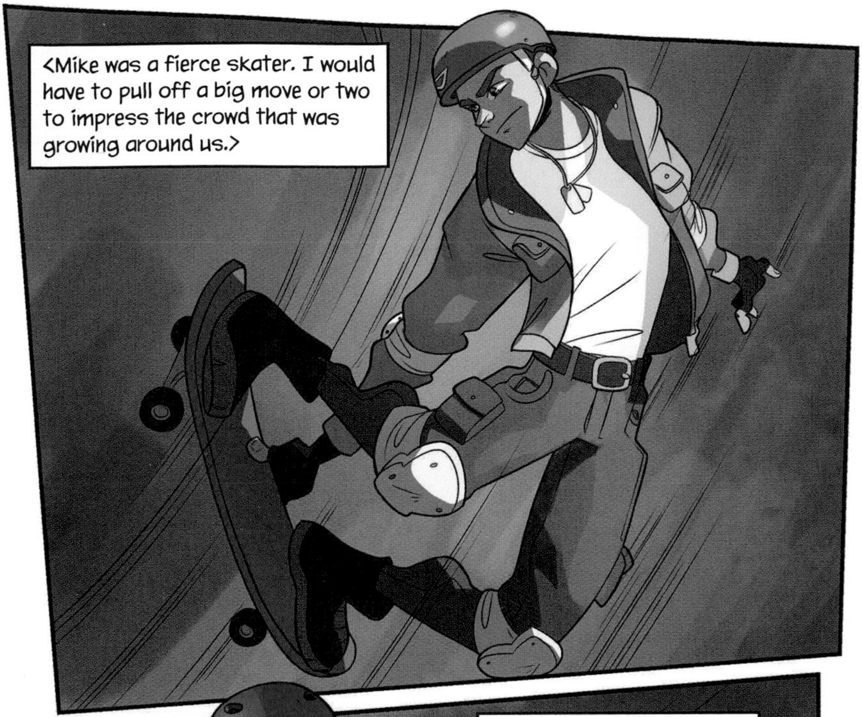
<Mike was a fierce skater. I would have to pull off a big move or two to impress the crowd that was growing around us.>

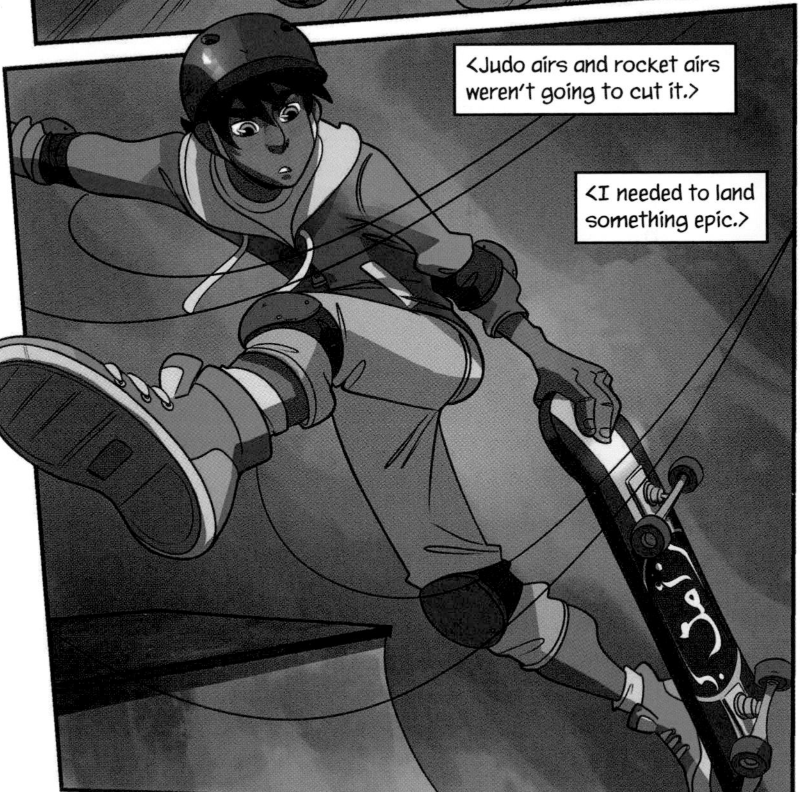
<Judo airs and rocket airs weren't going to cut it.>
<I needed to land something epic.>

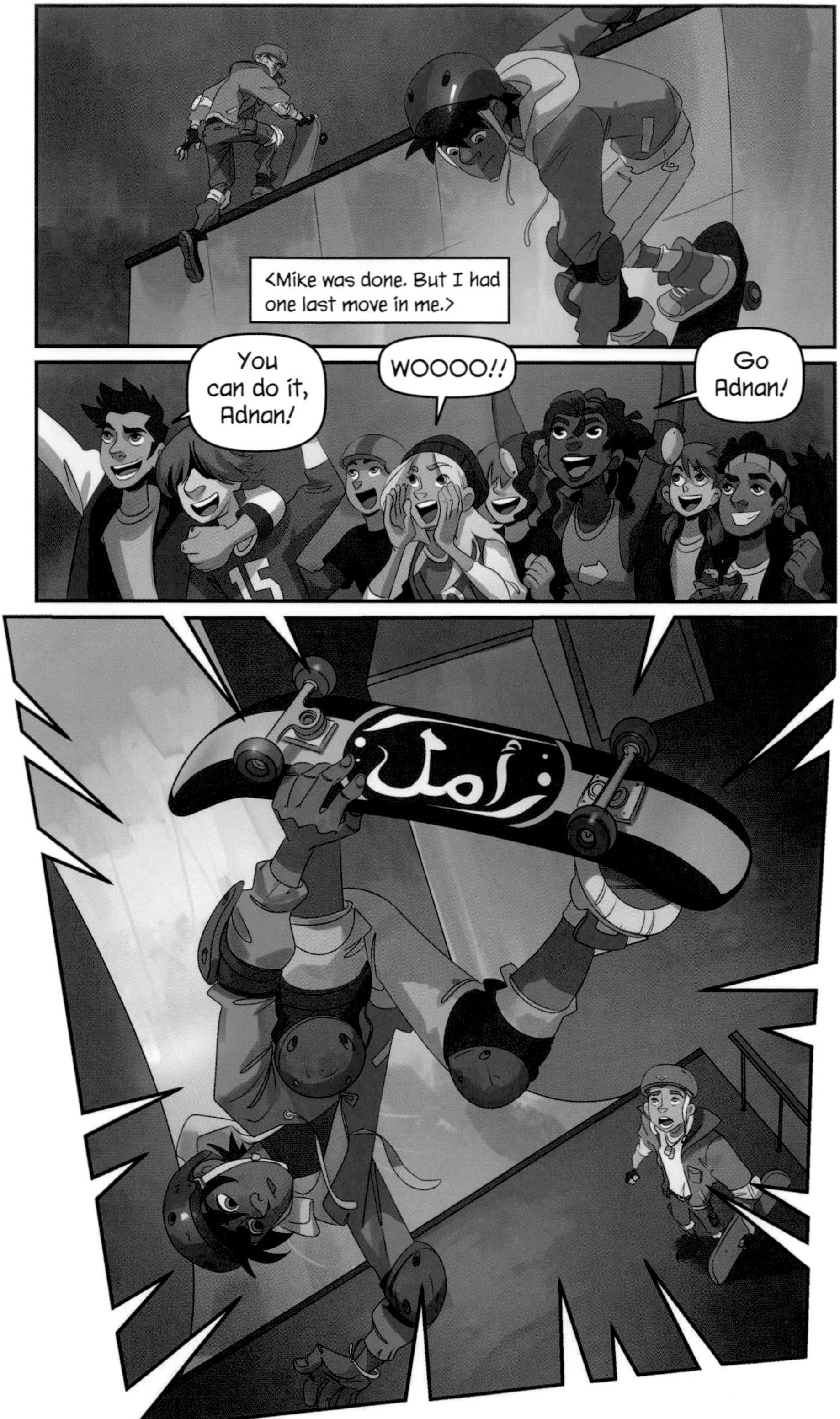
<Mike was done. But I had one last move in me.>
You can do it, Adnan!
WOOOO!!
Go Adnan!
أمل

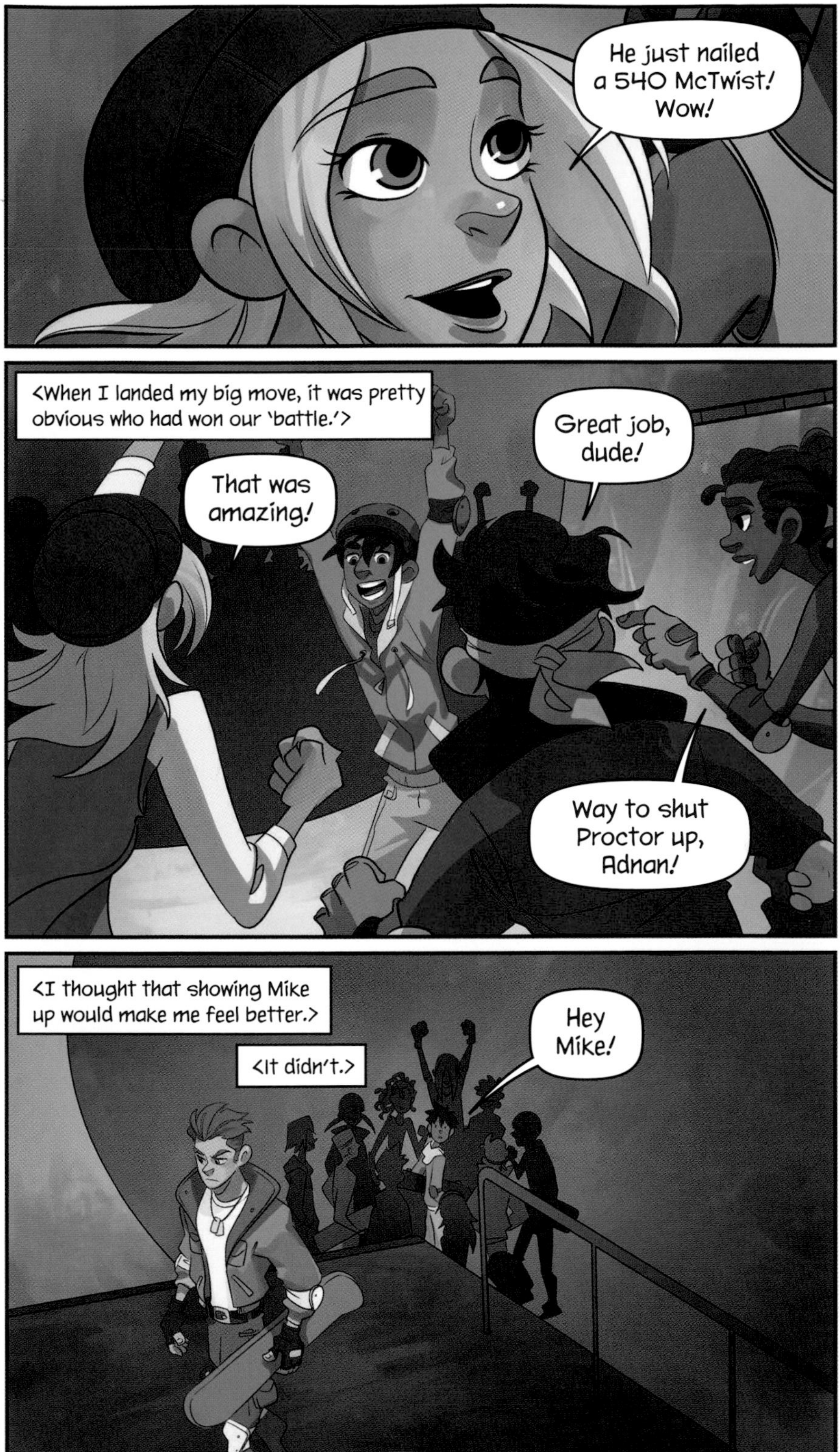
He just nailed a 540 McTwist! Wow!
<When I landed my big move, it was pretty obvious who had won our 'battle.'>
That was amazing!
Great job, dude!
Way to shut Proctor up, Adnan!
<I thought that showing Mike up would make me feel better.>
<It didn't.>
Hey Mike!

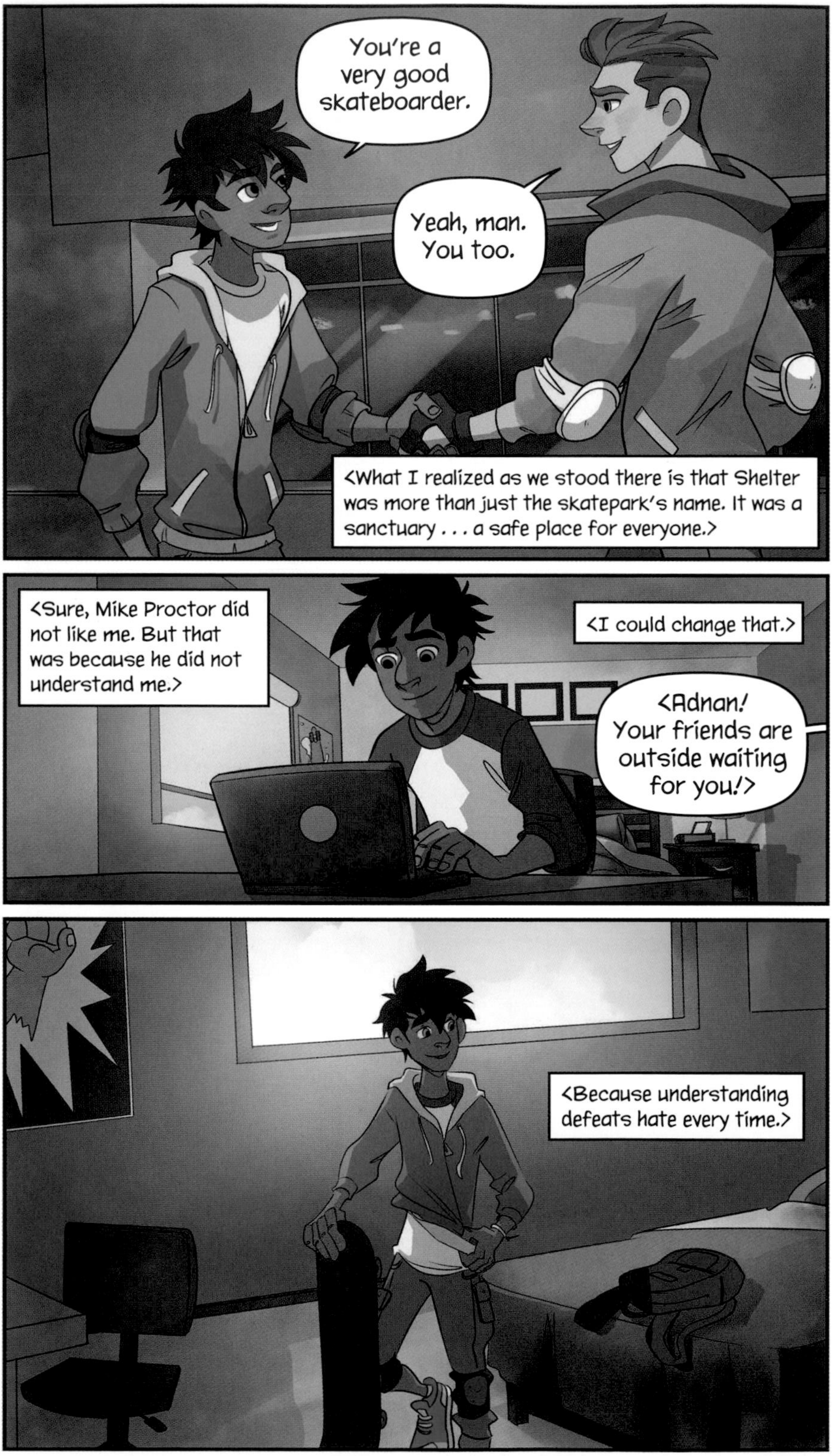
You're a very good skateboarder.
Yeah, man. You too.
<What I realized as we stood there is that Shelter was more than just the skatepark's name. It was a sanctuary . . . a safe place for everyone.>
<Sure, Mike Proctor did not like me. But that was because he did not understand me.>
<I could change that.>
<Adnan! Your friends are outside waiting for you!>
<Because understanding defeats hate every time.>

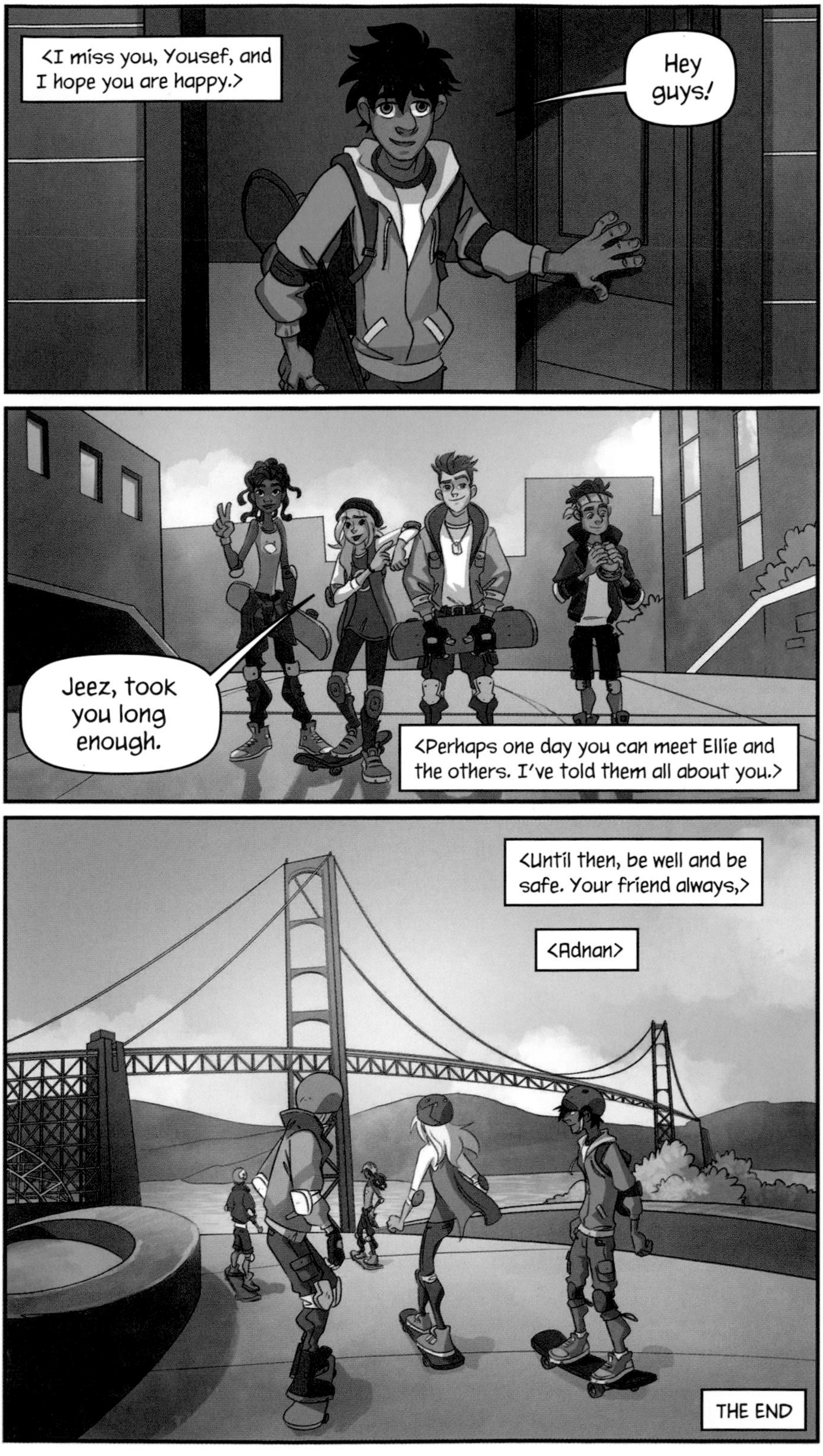
<I miss you, Yousef, and I hope you are happy.>
Hey guys!
Jeez, took you long enough.
<Perhaps one day you can meet Ellie and the others. I've told them all about you.>
<Until then, be well and be safe. Your friend always,>
<Adnan>
THE END

# VISUAL QUESTIONS

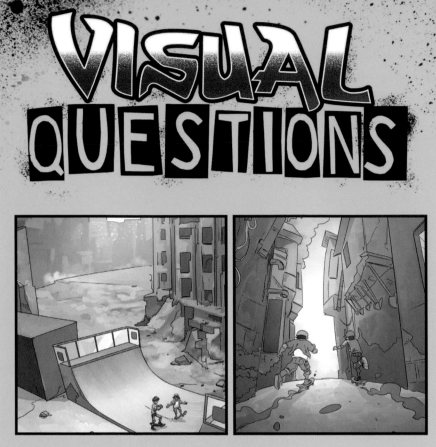

1. Graphic artists use background scenes to help tell a story. From the above panels, what can we learn about Adnan's home country by studying his surroundings?

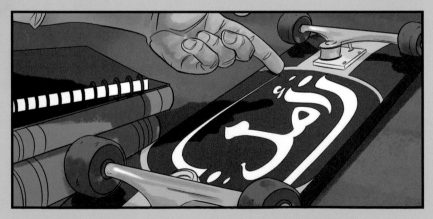

2. Adnan's skateboard has the Arabic symbol for the word "hope" painted on it. Why do you think this symbol is important for Adnan? Do you think it symbolizes something else that's important about the story?

3. Artists use closeups to show us what characters are thinking and feeling. Look at the panels below and describe what you think Adnan and Mike are thinking at this moment.

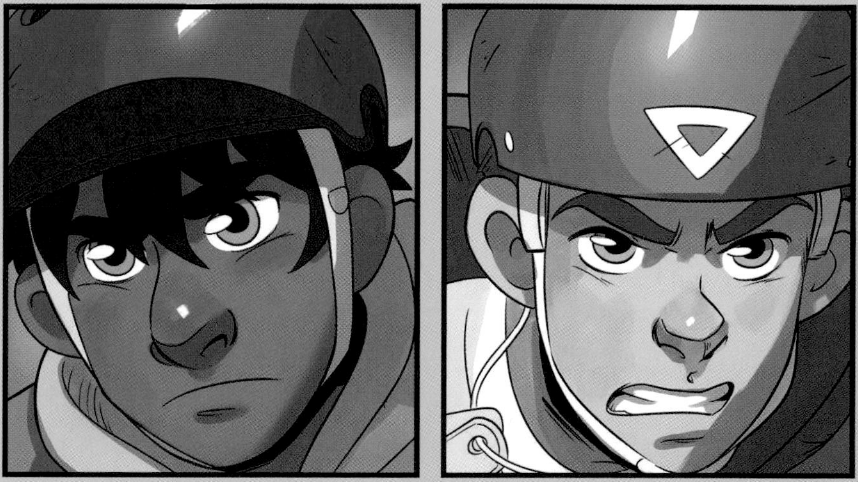

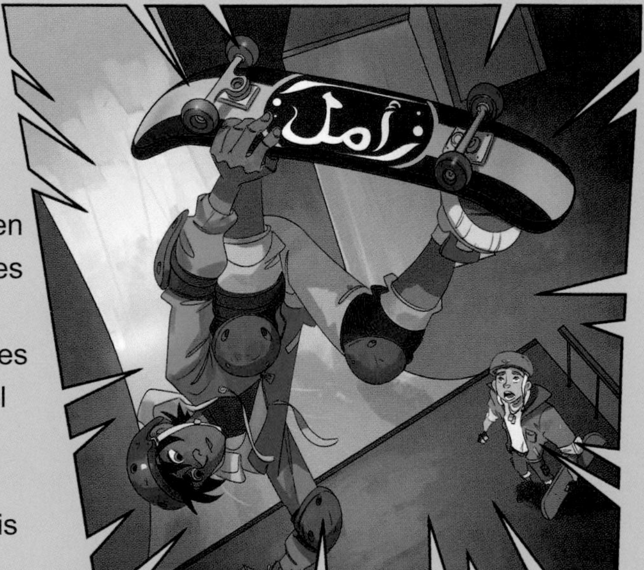

4. Graphic artists often use dramatic angles to show important moments. How does this dramatic panel impact the story? How would you choose to show this scene if you were the artist?

# SKATEBOARD FACTS

- The first skateboards were invented in the 1950s. Nobody knows who built the first skateboard, but early boards were nothing like today's models. They were simply wooden boards attached to roller skate wheels.

- Skateboarding first became popular in California with surfers who became known as 'sidewalk surfers.'

- In 1959 the 'Roller Derby Skateboard' was the first skateboard sold to the general public. Its wheels were made out of clay.

- The first skatepark in the world opened in Tucson, Arizona, on September 3, 1965.

- Frank Nasworthy added a substance called polyurethane to skateboard wheels in the 1970s. The substance made the wheels sleeker and faster, and the ride was less bumpy.

- Alan Ollie Gelfand was the first person to create a modern skateboarding trick in the 1970s. Today the basic 'ollie' is one of the first tricks that every skateboarder learns.

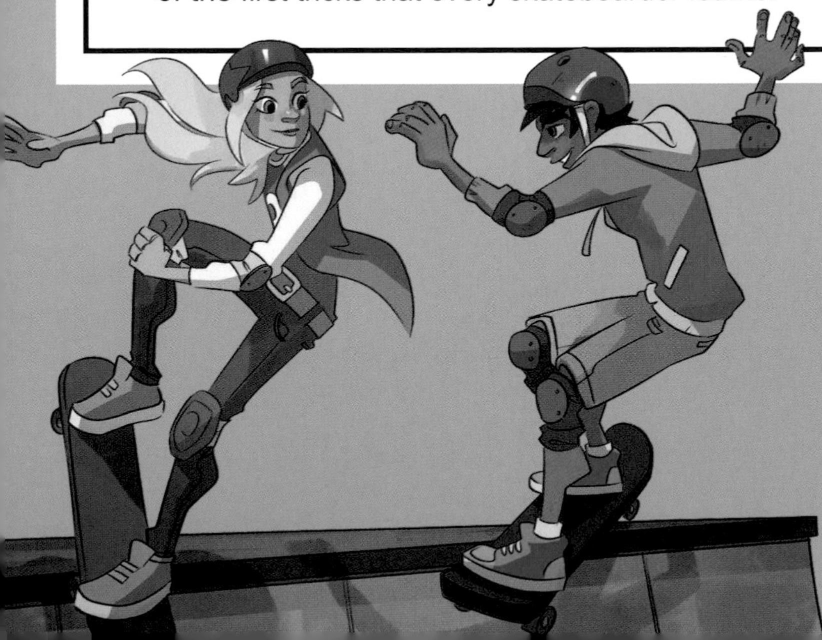

# SKATEBOARD WORDS TO KNOW

**BACKSIDE** — When a rider performs a trick with his or her back facing the ramp or obstacle.

**BOWL** — A concave ramp that goes around in a complete circle, forming a bowl shape.

**DECK** — The part of a skateboard that a rider stands on.

**FRONTSIDE** — When a rider performs a trick while facing forward toward a ramp or obstacle.

**HALF-PIPE** — A U-shaped ramp with high walls.

**JUDO AIR** — A trick in which the rider grabs the heel edge of the board with the front hand and kicks the front foot off the board while in the air.

**MCTWIST** — A complicated trick in which a rider performs a backside 540 while doing a front flip and lands riding forward.

**METHOD** — A trick in which a rider grabs the heel edge of the board and pulls it up toward his or her back.

**OLLIE** — A trick in which the rider smacks the tail of the board against the ground while the front foot pulls the board into the air to perform a hopping motion.

**ROCKET AIR** — A trick in which the rider grabs the front edge of the board with both hands and keeps his or her body as straight as possible while in the air to look like a rocket.

**TAILGRAB** — A trick in which the rider grabs the tail end of the board while in the air.

# GLOSSARY

**antics** (AN-tiks)—behavior meant to draw attention, often done in a foolish or ridiculous way

**distraction** (dih-STRAK-shuhn)—something that causes a person to lose focus on what he or she is doing

**epic** (EP-ik)—very large or impressive

**funk** (FUHNGK)—a depressed or dejected mood

**heritage** (HER-uh-tij)—the history and traditions handed down from one's family, ancestors, or country

**intimidate** (in-TIM-uh-date)—to frighten or threaten someone

**Neanderthal** (nee-AN-dur-thal)—an early type of human who lived more than 30,000 years ago

**perspective** (pur-SPEK-tiv)—the way things or events relate to each other in size or importance

**sanctuary** (SANGK-choo-er-ee)—a place that provides safety and protection to those in danger

**tactics** (TAK-tiks)—actions taken to achieve a goal

# READ THEM ALL!

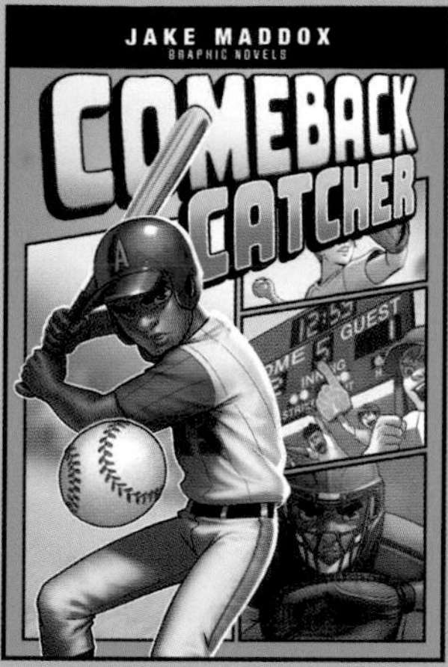
JAKE MADDOX
GRAPHIC NOVELS
COMEBACK CATCHER

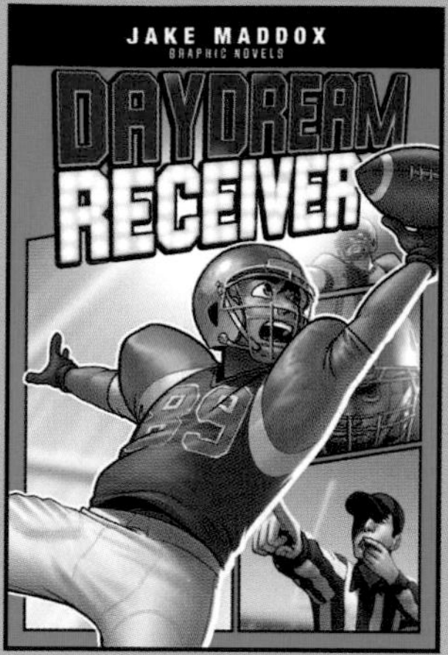
JAKE MADDOX
GRAPHIC NOVELS
DAYDREAM RECEIVER

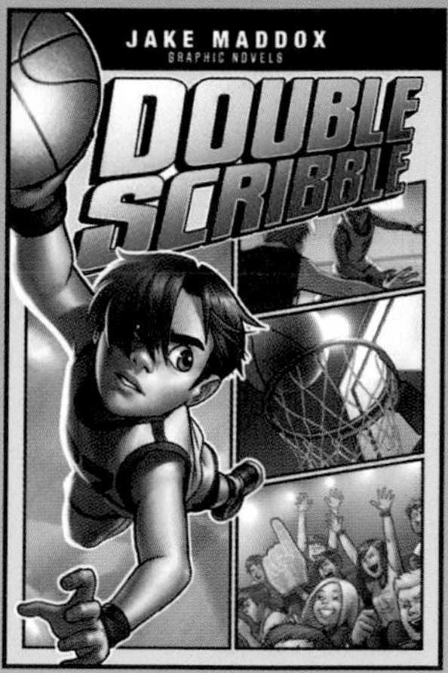
JAKE MADDOX
GRAPHIC NOVELS
DOUBLE SCRIBBLE

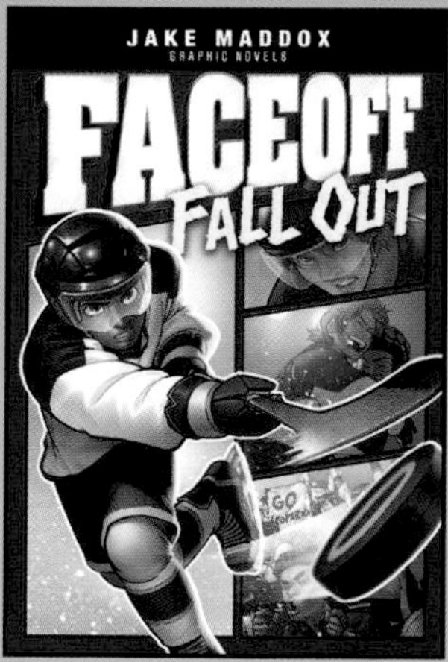
JAKE MADDOX
GRAPHIC NOVELS
FACEOFF FALL OUT

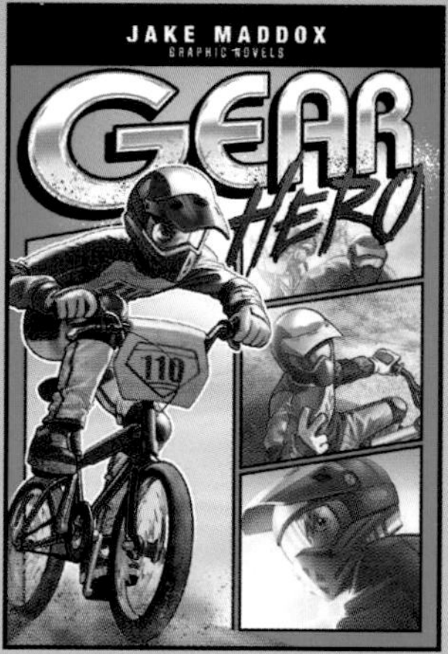
JAKE MADDOX
GRAPHIC NOVELS
GEAR HERO
110

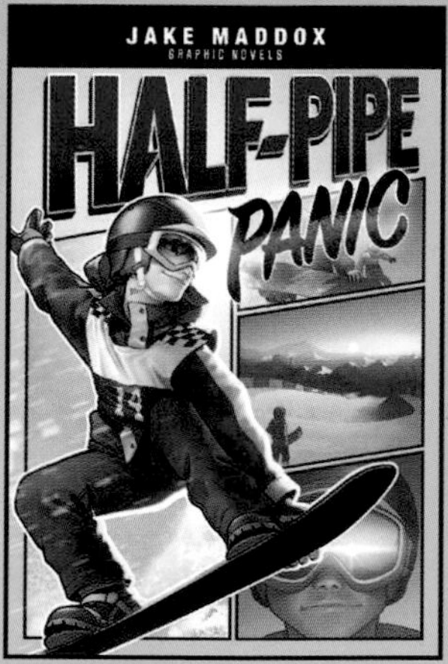
JAKE MADDOX
GRAPHIC NOVELS
HALF-PIPE PANIC

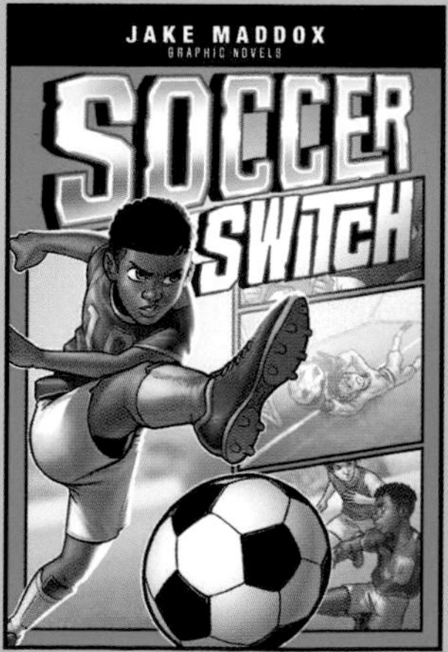
JAKE MADDOX
GRAPHIC NOVELS
SOCCER SWITCH

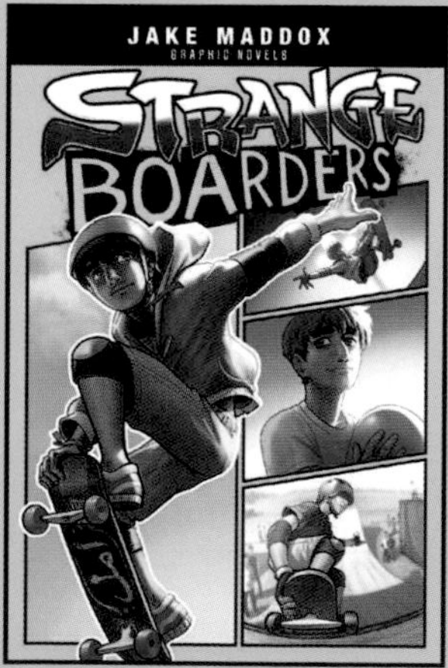
JAKE MADDOX
GRAPHIC NOVELS
STRANGE BOARDERS

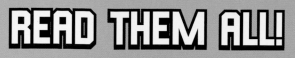

# ABOUT THE AUTHOR

**Brandon Terrell** is the author of numerous children's books, including several volumes in both the Tony Hawk 900 Revolution series and the Tony Hawk Live2Skate series. He has also written several Spine Shivers titles, and is the author of the Sports Illustrated Kids: Time Machine Magazine series. When not hunched over his laptop, Brandon enjoys watching movies and TV, reading, watching and playing baseball, and spending time with his wife and two children at his home in Minnesota.

# ABOUT THE ARTISTS

**Berenice Muñiz** is a Mexican artist from Monterrey. She has been drawing and coloring comics since 2009. Her work can be found on several children's books in her country, where she lives with her beloved partners in crime, a shaggy dog and four cats.

**Fares Maese** is a freelance artist. He has worked at Graphikslava as one of the founding members. He has also worked for Marvel Comics, Paizo Publishing, Games Workshop, and Legends of the Cryptics. He's been an illustrator for licences such as Warhammer, Star Wars, Wolverine, and the videogame Total War: Warhammer.

**Jaymes Reed** has operated the company Digital-CAPS: Comic Book Lettering since 2003. He has done lettering for many publishers, most notably and recently Avatar Press. He's also the only letterer working with Inception Strategies, an Aboriginal-Australian publisher that develops social comics with public service messages for the Australian government. Jaymes is also a 2012 and 2013 Shel Dorf Award Nominee.